Illustrations by Caleb Harrington

ISBN: 979-8-9902874-0-2

Cover design by Kelly Reilly and NightCafe Creator

First Edition: November 2024

Alaska Lost Boys Adventure

---

based on a true story

Kelly Reilly

Contents

I would like to thank the trio, Brandon, Josh and Todd who helped me remember so many details of the adventure.

My husband for many details about the rescue, and the bears.

I would also like to thank the following people for all the help I had writing my first book. There were so many edits and such great support from everyone. It was so much more fun sharing it with all of you.

Shiloh Butki, Cooper Butki, Tracy Silva, Lynn Harrington, Bri Kilbourne-Reilly, Ana Bernardino, Caleb Harrington, and Patricia Reilly

Introduction

Alaska Lost Boys Adventure has readers captivated at a life changing adventure in the woods of Alaska based on a true story. Three 12-yr old boys get lost in a blizzard and make decisions together to overcome predators and the harsh elements. The trio overcome their horrific situation and push through fears and cold with only bloody rabbits in a backpack to eat. With suspenseful wolf and brown bear encounters, dehydration, and a broken compass it will prove to be spellbinding. The boys are heroes of their own story and learn life lessons of teamwork, thinking ahead and evaluating with problem solving skills in a survival situation. The story is riveting to the end.

A teacher bonus section, discussion prompts, and a quiz all included.

A book for teachers and classrooms alike. Questions from children that will spark everyone's curiosity and learning. A sure to be hit!!!!!

Chapter One

FRIENDS

As the twelve-year-old boys huddled around the crackling fire to get warm, with snow falling around them, they wondered how they got lost. They had hunted rabbits in this area before and never got themselves turned around like this.

The day started out with such excitement, a birthday celebration for Will that promised thrills, adventure, and memories. The plan was straightforward. The boys, Will, Cooper and Henry had planned to go rabbit hunting down Swanson River Road near Mosquito Lake. A long, 20-mile dirt road, that ran north and south on the Kenai Peninsula. The boys grew up in Alaska, in the wild, but Swanson River Road was barren and there were no homes for 20 miles in any direction. A steep hilly terrain, with recent wildfires, which were ideal hunting grounds for rabbits. The new saplings that sprouted up close together as they grew provided cover for rabbits from hawks, owls, eagles, coyotes, wolves, bears and who knows what else, not to mention provided ample food to see them through the harsh Alaska winters.

Will's dad, Patrick, was a carpenter, and he loved to hunt and fish. It was what drew him to Alaska in the first place. It was known as "The Last Frontier," and he loved the adventure of it. His three older brothers and younger sister along with his parents had also moved to Alaska. It is just as they say, majestic, wild and beautiful.

Patrick was working near the hunting grounds area earlier in the week and had gone for a short drive down Swanson River Road. While driving around he spotted numerous rabbits for a few miles up and down the usually barren dirt road. He went back the next day to solidify the findings.

On Wednesday evening as Patrick arrived home from work, he went straight to find Will.

"Hey, there are so many rabbits down Swanson River Road right now we should take advantage of it. It only happens about every 10 years. Why don't you call Coop and Henry, and we can go Saturday."

"Really" Will responded. "Ya, I'll call them. How long can we go and what time can we get them?"

"Well, we need to go early, and I need to work a little on Saturday right near there. So...how about pick up around 6:30 am done hunting by noon and afterward we can go get hamburgers for your birthday. Boys should be home by 3." Patrick added.

Will ran to the house and got on the phone. He emerged back out in the yard after about 15 mins. "Henry just got a new gun he is super excited, and Coop can go too."

"Good. It's a plan then." His dad replied.

The rabbits would be great for the freezer for winter rabbit stew with vegetables, potatoes, and gravy. The rabbit population was up so going rabbit hunting right now was a good idea due to the ecological cycle of overpopulation of the rabbits about every 10 years. The rabbits would be plentiful for a time and deplete their food source due to their overpopulation. Then the rabbit population would die, which in turn affected thc predators that ate them, like coyotes, wolves, owls, hawks, bears, etc. Then the predators would not have enough of a food source to survive, and they would dwindle in population due to the lack of food which for them was the rabbit population. The cycle would take about 10 years to come back around.

The hunting would be straight forward, a perfect outing. So, the boys planned to go on Saturday for just a couple of hours.

On Saturday morning Patrick and Will jumped in the old truck and headed to pick up the other two boys, Henry and Cooper. Patrick had to go to work on a house near Swanson River Road for just a few hours and would swing back and pick the boys up on the way home.

The families had all been friends for a long time. Will and Cooper had met in Kindergarten and Will and Henry had grown up together since birth. Henry lived about 2 miles from Will down a dirt road in a log cabin. He lived with his parents and had an older Sister. Henry had blond wispy light hair, a linebacker's build, a pleasant demeanor, and a boisterous laugh that often came at inopportune times. Usually, because he found other people funny, they just couldn't keep up with him. He was logical and reasonable. Little did he know his logic and reason would be put to the test in the Alaska wilderness. Henry's dad, Charles was a small engine mechanic who owned his own shop. Henry's mom, Grace taught music at the elementary school. Henry wore a Denver Broncos sweatshirt, fall jacket, Carhart's and hiking shoes.

Will knocked on the door. Knock. Knock. Knock. And **BOOM** Henry swung the door open and as quick as a flash was through the door and headed to the truck.

"Let's go," he yelled, "What are we waiting for your mom?"

Will chuckled and took off after him. "I thought you were going to show me your new girly 20 gauge first." He loved Henry's enthusiasm, and he was always full of energy for hunting, fishing, camping, or football. Near the the truck, they checked their guns and made sure they were unloaded and had safety's on. Patrick, who was known to be a mellow laid-back guy, but aggressively insisted on safety when it came to your guns.

"You checked those guns again, right!" He yelled when they got into the back seat.

"Yes sir," both boys quickly responded but returned to their ogling of Henry's new gun. It was brilliant.

It was only October, and the full weight of an Alaskan winter had not come down on them yet. A perfect time to go hunting, as the Snowshoe hare's fur coats started to turn white to blend in with the snow, however they had not had a snow yet. The animals' fur coats started to turn right around the first frost and that had certainly come and gone. The white of the hare's fur made them easier to spot in the dense underbrush where they would be hunting.

Will, Henry and Cooper had been fishing and hunting since they were very small. All three families were very adept at hunting and fishing the Alaska outdoors. Will and Cooper met in kindergarten. However, Will and Henry had grown up together since they were infants.

A few miles down the road, Cooper's family lived on a large homestead with several small log cabins spread evenly about the ocean front property; the smoke swirling up into the sky from the wood stove telling Will and Henry that Cooper was home and staying warm. The ocean view was spectacular from here.

Cooper was a handsome Alaska native with dark hair and brown eyes. Known for his ability to make everyone feel at ease with his bright and pleasing smile. He was equally skilled at hunting and fishing like the other two boys. Cooper worked on his dad's commercial fishing boat every summer and his grip and arms showed it. Bob, Cooper's dad grew up on a homestead in North Kenai and passed on his fishing expertise and love of the great outdoors. Cooper had two sisters and a brother. Nan, Cooper's mother, worked at the local electric company. Cooper had on blue jeans and a winter coat, but what was immediately apparent as he trotted down the steps of the porch toward the truck was that he was wearing snow boots that were too big for his feet.

Cooper, hopped into the front cab of the truck next to Patrick. "Hey Coop, ready to get some rabbits," Patrick said excitedly hoping to build the excitement up for the three boys.

"You know it Pat," Coop said as if the two had been old friends.

Will and Henry couldn't take it and burst out laughing. "What are you wearing," Will asked?

Henry quickly chimed in with, "you aren't going to be able to walk a half mile in those cement blocks."

"Shut up" Cooper replied, "I couldn't find my tennis shoes. I think Josh wore them to my uncles last night and now I can't find them." Josh was

Coopers younger brother and was known to "borrow" his things.

Will liked the outdoors, but mostly because his friends and father did. He loved hunting and fishing but the killing part of it never sat right with him. However, fishing and hunting were part of his everyday life as well. His family had a cabin on the Kenai River along with a small motorboat. They fished in the summer for the famous Kenai River King salmon. His dad would trek into the woods hiking and trapping even in the winter. His mother, Junie, in her spare time, made hats, baby boots and gloves from muskrat, mink, rabbits, and bear hides almost anything they brought home. Will went with his dad on the trap lines and to the beaver pond below his house to learn and explore. There were always animal tracks to be found, bears, beavers, river otters, coyotes, wolves and more. He was taught trapping skills, skinning, and winter survival along with knowledge of the dangers in the woods of Alaska in the winter. A compass was part of their journeys, and he learned how to use it and read the sky for directions. Will had two sisters and a baby brother. Will had brown hair, green eyes and a muscular build. He also excelled in sports and school. He wore his regular fall clothing of a long-sleeved T-shirt, blue jeans, tennis shoes and an insulated raincoat to go rabbit hunting.

Basic survival skills and bear safety were just everyday lessons. The knowledge of guns and of Alaska's dangers were essential. Boy's growing up in a small town In Alaska had to have knowledge of the harsh elements. It didn't matter if it was winter or summer. Ice would melt off the lakes and ponds at different rates and falling through the ice was a real threat. Raging rivers and frigid temperatures of the waters in Alaska even in the summer generated high death rates for drowning either by hypothermia or failure to wear a life vest. Then there was the threat of the animals. Bears kill and maim people every year. But, Moose cause more injuries to people than bears. Moose were very prevalent where the boys lived and more encounters than they can name happened to each one of them. If you lived in Alaska, you had a moose story.

Will remembered he would walk across the trail to his grandma's house, and he was taught to actively watch for moose, if they were on the trail, you got off! The moose would not get off a trail and the boys learned that at a young age. In the winter moose did not hesitate to attack even trucks if it was a year of deep snow, and they were hungry and angry about being forced off a plowed road into deep snow. They would attack and kick anything they took as a threat, so they were even more unpredictable in the winter. They were known to try and stand down trains.

As the trio embarked on their rabbit-hunting adventure, little did they know that their familiarity with the Alaskan wilderness and its challenges would be put to the test.

Chapter Two

HUNTING GROUNDS

The boys were buzzing with excitement to get to the rabbit hunting grounds. It was almost an hour drive. The excitement was building as they drove further and further down the long dirt road. The sun was just coming up in the distance, a hazy red and orange glow on the horizon. It now seems like it could have been a warning looking back. They were not prepared for what was about to happen; they had no snacks or water and nothing to hold water. They expected to only be in the woods for a couple hours and then hike back to the truck to meet Patrick and head home.

It was mid-October in Alaska and the perfect time to spot rabbits easily with the leaves gone from the trees and bushes. The forest was less dense, and mosquitoes were dead for the season so they would not have to fight that.

Their destination was Swanson River Road near Mosquito Lake where Patrick had spotted the rabbits earlier in the week. There was a sign marking Mosquito Lake which was the landmark his dad knew would be the best starting point and easy to use as a meeting point later in the day. When he spotted the Mosquito Lake sign, they pulled over off the road and parked the truck. This was it the rabbit's paradise. All the boys jumped out talking excitedly and grabbed their jackets and guns.

Patrick before leaving reminded them, "The most dangerous things out here are not the bears and not the moose, it is you making mistakes. Be careful with your guns and pay attention to where you are.

The sun rises where, Henry," he asked?

Henry replied as if to a drill sergeant, "In the east, sir"!

"Cooper where does the sun set"?

"In the North," Cooper jokingly responded. Pat shot him a look like he was not messing around. "In the West, in the west, sir"!

"That's more like it." Pat said sternly with a crook of a smile forming. Patrick really liked these boys and enjoyed them more and more as their wit and humor expanded.

"Will where is the compass?" he continued his questioning. Will grabbed at his fanny pack, which wasn't a cool clothing item, he knew, and Cooper and Henry gave him a lot of guff for it, but it was extremely useful.

"Brought your purse I see." giggled Henry.

"Let me see it." Pat stated. Will opened the red fanny pack and showed him the compass. "Good, now where are your knives?" The boys all quickly produced blades of all different shapes and sizes. Will had a big hunting knife for skinning. Cooper had a Swiss army knife, useful for just about everything and Henry produced a 4" pocketknife. "Ok, not bad, but where are your matches?" The boys all produced some form of matches that appeared to be protected from moisture. Pat was just about to ask about the prospect of a lighter, but a bald eagle flew over them and landed in a nearby tree with a wing expansion unmeasurably majestic. They all became distracted, and Patrick never asked about a lighter.

"Wow, do you see that?" Patrick remarked pointing at the eagle. "That guy is huge," He is also here for those rabbits, I can guarantee it."

"We see those guys at the beach all the time," said Cooper "All of them looking for fish guts, and the gulls take the leftovers. The eagle's rule."

They all looked quickly at the sky. It was clear, and the sun was coming up in the east. It was a beautiful day, the air was crisp, if not freezing and the views were astonishing. A wonderful day to go hunting. Or so they thought.

Before Patrick left, they discussed the plan for meeting after hunting and for final confirmation of pickup. They would hunt to the West of the road, so if they didn't walk more than 10 miles in either direction, they could walk out and hit the dirt road walking East. It was not going to be a problem when it was time to walk back out, because they had the sun, and they had a compass.

"I will be right here at this sign with the truck about noon give or take a minute." Pat said. "What do your watches all say now?"

"Mine is at 8," said Will

"Yep" said Coop, "Me too."

Patrick explained to them before he jumped in the truck to leave them: "in Alaska, in October the sun rising in the east moves low across the southern sky and sets directly west. The directions are easier to assess because the further North you are the lower the sun is in the southern sky at noon. So, be smart and pay attention to the guns and each other and I will see you in a few hours."

"We got it!" Will shot back

"See ya later." Henry replied.

"We won't be stupid." Coop answered as Patrick drove away.

As the boys entered the woods, the crunching ground beneath them was a familiar and comforting sound. They spread out about 10-15 yards in a line to walk through the brush to scare up rabbits. As

Will entered the dense forest he had a funny feeling about it, and he glanced back at the road. He shrugged it off and ducked his shoulder into the wall of foliage pushing through to get to those rabbits. The saplings and brush raked across his face, and immediately he noticed his insulated raincoat was tearing. It might be a cold couple of hours, but nothing he couldn't handle – he was an Alaskan after all.

Navigating the dense woods was always a challenge. The place they walked into was an old burn area. There was a ton of deadfall (deadfall are fallen trees) in this area because of the burn. The tundra was soft, wet, and very uneven so the boys had to watch their steps to avoid tripping. But being young men, they could maneuver quickly through the woods fueled by youthful energy and adrenaline. They were unfazed with the brush and branches hitting their faces or pulling their hair. They crashed through the underbrush like it was nothing. They were loudly and excitedly talking about the rabbits, school, girls, and what they were going to do the rest of the day. They had walked less than a 1/4 mile when they started spotting the rabbits. They crashed through the underbrush to flush out the rabbits.

"C'mon let's go." said Henry, "Geez, you guys are slow, my mom is hoping for some rabbit stew for tomorrow."

"My grandpa loves it too," said Coop "I need at least three today for me."

"Three?" replied Will "I'm hoping for eight or more for me."

"I thought you didn't like to shoot the bunnies," said Henry towards Will sarcastically.

"I don't always, but my grandma asked me for some as well." Will replied.

"We always have so many fish all winter that a few rabbits are a nice change at my house." Cooper continued.

"There!" pointing at rabbits, Henry snapped his fingers and shushed them to alert the others as to not scare the rabbits he just spotted.

"Line!" Will shot back. The trio quickly adjusted to keep distance between each other and made a line so as not be in "the line of fire." Yelling, "Line!" while hunting with multiple hunters kept the boys alert to the placement of each of them and back in a safe zone behind or equal to the line of the shooter. Trying to remember gun safety and not get caught up in the excitement. Henry shot a rabbit and threw it in the backpack.

"Me next" Cooper yelled trying to get his turn.

"Ya, ya," said Will. "We can both shoot next, just keep the line and Coop you shoot rabbits way left and I will take right then there is no crossfire. The boys knew to yell and communicate while shooting rabbits together to keep it safe.

As they continued Henry spoke up "So, you guys know these aren't called rabbits, right? They are called Snowshoe hares. Look it up,"

"Ya, but it's so easy to say" responded Will. "Let's go shoot some hares, sounds dumb."

Coop chimed in, "Let's get some rabbits sounds way better than let's go get some hares, that totally doesn't work. Besides, no one really cares if it's hare stew or rabbit stew and hare stew sounds like you're eating someone's hair." Will kept talking. "Just sounds wrong."

"The rabbits, real cottontail rabbits are in Southeast Alaska." Henry informed. "Real rabbits are way smaller, skinnier, with shorter legs and their babies are born hairless and blind."

"Good, we can eat hares up here and eat larger and better stew and we call 'em rabbits. Who cares?" said Coop. "Hare stew won't catch on Henry."

"Also," Henry added to finish his thoughts like he didn't hear the other two. "Hares have nests above ground not burrows like regular rabbits. Hares are faster, have larger ears and are born with fur and with their eyes open." Then Henry finished with. "You guys should probably know this stuff."

Coop rolled his eyes behind Henry who couldn't see him.

The trio now moved slowly forward flushing out more rabbits and watching underbrush for activity. After they shot the rabbits, they shoved them into a Minnie Mouse backpack that Will grabbed from the house, which was his sister's, because he did not want to take the time to find his. Besides, they were only going to be gone a short while and she would not even know it was gone.

Moving forward, they scanned for more rabbits, and time slipped away. It was a couple of hours into the adventure when they were ready to turn back the sky had clouded over, and it was impossible to see which way was East. The sun was gone due to the heavy cloud cover. The compass came out of the pack. Without hesitation, they went due east the way the compass was telling them. The thrill of the hunt had made for a great day but would soon be overshadowed by the unexpected twist of the journey they were about to have in the Alaska wilderness.

Chapter Three

THE THREE BEAR RULE

The boys walked for about an hour and a half talking and laughing about school and girls and sports once again.

"So, Henry, Katie is all over you for math help in class. Are you sure it's just math help she wants?" Will jeered.

Cooper jumped in, "Oooh, its more than math help she wants, Henry just is slow to figure it out." they all laughed.

"Yeah, Well, Will has Claire chasing and stalking him and he doesn't like her because she's too smart for him, isn't that right Will?" Henry came back.

"You wish. She's my sister's friend, "No thanks."

At one point, they paused for a break, and as Henry looked down, he screamed "Snap! Look at this!" he pointed at fresh bear tracks and scat (scat is feces or bodily waste in solid form). He called the other boys over to come take a look and as they all looked down, awestruck they went silent. An adrenaline surge went through each of their bodies. The kind where you could hear your blood pumping in your ears so loud you couldn't hear for a few seconds. The boys knew the difference between black bear scat and brown bear scat.

"Those are brown bear tracks," Cooper said. "Which means it's also brown bear scat!"

"Yeah, duh, and no chance those are from a black bear either." said Will.

Henry, nodded in agreement, "yea you're right, you can see the claw marks are like 2" from the toepads. **That** is a big bear." A quietness crept over the forest, and their moods.To confirm their fears, they examined the fresh pile of scat, it was still warm, and the heat vapors could be seen at the right angle. Brown bear scat being very large, about two inches wide, tubular and it had small bones in it, possibly rabbit fur, maybe mice or shrew bones and fur. Henry picked up a stick and began prodding the pile.

"That's moose fur in this pile." Henry noticed.

"He may have a moose down somewhere protecting and eating off it. Moose season just ended." Will added.

"Ya, there could be various piles of moose guts or other things hunters have left out here for him to eat." Henry continued.

Cooper kicked at it in fear and frustration. "It takes a big bear to take down a moose. Come and get us you son of a gun," he said as confidently as he could muster.

He kicked the scat, and it burst all over the place. They all knew what they were looking at and knew what it meant.

"These tracks are headed dead east, right where we have to go. What do you guys want to do? Will questioned his friends. "Should we go around and hit the road at a different point and walk up the road to find my dad?

"What if the bear changed direction slightly and we walk right into it? Wherever it was it could be over the next hill or behind the next tree." Cooper added.

"These tracks are heading the same way we are. We could go around and hope we don't go the wrong way or keep going right behind him and hope his path turns." Henry said!

"Either way if we guess wrong it could be around the next bend no matter what we choose." Will continued "Well, we have guns, and ammunition and we will shoot it if attacks us."

But Henry the ever reasonable and thoughtful one found the flaw in their plan, "I have a 20 gauge, you have a 12 gauge, and Cooper has a 22 that are loaded for rabbits, not bears the size of a house. My 20 gauge will only make it mad."

Will nodded, but Cooper wouldn't have any of it, he needed something to soothe his fears. "What do you mean these guns won't work?"

"Both shotguns have shells that are loaded with small BBs meant for rabbits, they would barely penetrate the skin of a brown bear," Henry said way too calmly for Will.

"Wait a second," Will rummaged through his fanny pack.

"What magic wand do you have in that girl purse that you think is going to save us from a brown bear?" Cooper said trying to hide the fear in his voice.

Will finished rifling through his fanny pack, as if a magician in a show he waived his hands back and forth saying "ta da," as he revealed his find. He had a 12-gauge shotgun shell.

"I thought shotgun shells would barely penetrate the skin," Cooper said disappointedly.

"No, this isn't any shotgun shell, it's a slug, specifically for a bear." Will said victoriously. Henry smiled big and then as if a dark cloud overcame his jubilation made an "Ugh" sound.

"Wait, what did I miss?" Cooper asked.

Henry explained his change in mood, "One shot, we have one shot with a shotgun and a slug to fend off a huge brown bear, that is trying to fatten up before hibernation or could be in a really bad mood!"

"It's better than nothing," Will shot back. "Let's wait until he gets close."

"I am not waiting for anything to get that close, my god, that thing is going to eat us alive, ya, no way, **I am running**, and you two can wait for it to get close," Cooper said unapologetically. He wouldn't be waiting around to make sure that Will hit a HUGE moving target with fangs with one bullet while they were all standing around waiting to see what happens.

"How about this?" Henry stopped the discussion from rolling into an argument. "Here's the plan, I will shoot the 20 gauge in the air several times to scare it away, if that doesn't work and it comes for us, I'll turn the gun on the bear, every little bit could make the difference. Cooper, you use your .22 and aim for the eyes, Will, you wait for it to get close enough so that you can guarantee you hit it dead center with that slug." Henry's voice was gaining courage as he unraveled the plan. "Whoever takes the shot, should be brave enough to wait for the bear to get close enough to guarantee a hit."

Then Cooper added in, "To maximize the chance that we hit it at least, we should aim for center mass."

They reasoned that a wounded bear might take off or at least be easier to run from...which brought up the final point of discussion.

"There will be no more talk of running from this bear, we will fight it with everything we have." Will ended the conversation with that. "All three of us will take a shot at the monster."

"I like it," Henry said. "Probably our best bet you can't outrun him."

"You got that right!" Will commented.

"I don't like it," Cooper said shaking his head, "but it's better than nothing."

They were each picturing the kind of beast that would leave a track that large. Henry walked about ten feet to the right and put his hand on a large birch tree, a type of tree that is known for being hard wood, and he ran his fingers down the 14" long sweeping scratch marks on it at above his head. "Oh ****," Henry was now cursing which wasn't like him at all. His eyes drifted up towards the top of the tree and his eyes got wide as they all took in the marks 5 feet above their heads.

"Geez, its huge, look at this!" said Henry

Will visualized the bear coming down a hill at them tearing through the underbrush and commented. "I've seen small trees torn through in patches while hunting with my dad and it was a scary sight." He continued, "I can see Henry shooting unsuccessfully trying to deter the bear, Cooper's 22 bouncing off the beast as it charges us." Even in his imagination it was terrifying. "As long as we don't get buck fever trying to shoot that bear, we may be ok." Will said.

It was tough to keep the cool calm demeanor it takes to make a good shot, and they may have to do it while the bear is charging.

"Buck fever" or what his dad told him was built up excitement and nervousness that would spike adrenaline causing a hunter to shake and miss a target.

Each of the boys had experienced a bit of "buck fever" today while hunting rabbits and made their mistakes, but now they felt like pros, at least when it came to rabbits. A brown bear attack would give rise to the same feelings and mistakes as before. They wanted out of the area and to get back to the truck. They all got quiet and looked around nervously and quickened their steps.

They had been trained to make noise and talk while hiking through the woods, which they had been doing to scare bears. However, when faced with the sighting of those paw prints of such a potentially large bear no one spoke for quite some time. They knew that the guns they carried for rabbits would not be helpful in defense of a brown bear should they come upon it.

In Will's mind, he went over and over the things his father had told him about bear tracks. "I'm pretty sure those were brown bear tracks." Will spoke out loud "With brown bear or a grizzly bear the wide, straight toes and forward-set claw prints signaled a brown bear. That's what the prints appeared to be. Right?" Will somewhat asking for confirmation. "If the toes were more rounded down on the outside edges of the paw and claw prints were closer to the toes or nonexistent and much smaller, it would be a black bear." Will evaluated out loud. "Right?" Will continued, but Will was sure it was a brown bear.

"Ya, no doubt about it." Then Henry started talking a little nervously to break the silence, "Hey, so you guys do know the difference between a brown bear and a grizzly bear? A grizzly bear lives in the interior of Alaska, and the brown bear lives on the coast. They are named differently but are essentially the same. The diet of the brown bear and the grizzly is the only difference. The brown bear is bigger because his diet consists of salmon he can access near the water. But people assume the grizzly is bigger just because the name sounds scarier but that's not altogether true. We live on the Kenai Peninsula and the coastal bear is named the brown bear. And a large brown bear can be up to 10 feet in length and weigh 1200 lbs." Henry was talking into the woods now assuming the other two weren't listening.

But Cooper replied, "Your babbling Henry besides Brown bear or grizzly bear it doesn't matter, they are massive creatures, and I don't want to see one today."

Will shot back to show he was listening too, "And yes we do know the difference, Henry." They were all a bit nervous and agitated from the sight of tracks.

Will's dad had shown him many times what black bear scat looked like behind their house near the beaver pond. The scat changes with the seasonal diet. The leaves, insects, and grasses can turn it green and tubular in the summer. In the late season it gets looser and larger with berries and fish. Black bear scat is much smaller than brown bear scat.

Will broke in with his information so as not to appear ignorant. "My dad would tell us about the rules for bears and if he wasn't telling us my mom would lecture over and over if we were picking berries. In Alaska **the three-bear rule is If it's black fight back. If it's brown lie down. If it's white, say goodnight!** When or if you kids were to see a bear, he most likely will have already smelled you and will want to avoid you and go the other way if it's a normal bear. But, if it approaches, **DO NOT RUN! Slowly back away and if that still doesn't work apply the 3-bear rule.** Geez, I can repeat it just like my mom, yikes!"

Cooper jumped in to take a turn with his knowledge, "Yep that's the **3 Bear Rule** we all hear it. We get the lecture down at the beach during subsistence on the homestead." He continued. "If it's a black bear, make yourself look large and loud and fight back with sticks or rocks or whatever you find. If it's a brown bear, play dead, "If it's brown lie down," and cover your neck and curl your knees up to protect your stomach. Finally, the white "say Goodnite" means its a polar bear and you're just dead! NO escape." Cooper went on, "Polar bears are not on the Kenai but in Holy Cross way up north my family sees them quite a bit."

The trio had quickened their pace. This wasn't fun anymore and the stakes had been raised.

Henry reminded them "Well, if by chance you are carrying bloody rabbits, like us, they may get curious and follow you. Not sure if there's a rule for that.

Chapter Four

LOST

Henry broke the silence saying, "Shouldn't we have hit the road by now?" Where was the road?

Will replied "Ya, I think we are just walking at an angle or something through this brush. The road has that curve in it below the sign where my dad should be waiting. We must be barely missing it and somewhat parallel with it?"

"We've been heading east long enough to have intersected with the road at some point." stated Will. They all were feeling it and were shoving the fear down deep with their disbelief that they may be LOST.

"Keep walking, just keep walking." Henry said. He looked down at his watch and blurted out "We have been walking for three hours." The sighting of the brown bear scat and tracks distracted them, and they did not realize how much time had passed and now it was starting to slowly snow.

"Geez, you're kidding. Now it's snowing, of course it's snowing." Cooper remarked to no one in particular.

"Are you reading that thing right," Henry interrupted motioning for the compass to be passed to him. Cooper pushed over to Henry and the two peered down at the compass. "It looks like we're going the right way." Said Henry.

"I can read a compass Henry." Will retorted.

"Well," said Henry "It feels like we should have hit the road a while ago."

"We must have gone farther than we thought," Will said,

Cooper broke in, "I am not sure how much further I can go; these boots are killing me. My legs are starting to feel like they want to cramp, and I'm thirsty."

It was true Cooper had been pulling up the rear and seemed to be struggling to keep up. It was hard country, and they picked an even harder country to be hunting in, where the rabbits were. The fact that the first blizzard of the year started exactly when they decided to head back was just bad luck.

"Henry confirmed "the compass is reading east and there's no sun to help us, so keep walking." Henry and Cooper both had looked at the compass, how could they all be reading it wrong?

Will began thinking out loud "We must be walking just enough at an angle that we still haven't hit the road, and we aren't hearing any road traffic." He went on, "But, in the middle of October on a Saturday traffic would be minimal on Swanson River Road anyway."

It was true it was still too cloudy to get a direction from the sky. Growing up the boys were taught if you get lost you should stay put and not make things worse. Should they stay put? Were they really lost? No, they were headed in the right direction they all agreed, sort of. No one mentioned "staying put" especially after they stumbled across those bear tracks.

"Stupid clouds, stupid snow!" Cooper spouted out of frustration.

"What is happening," repeated Henry, "Surely we should be at the road." He wasn't listening to the others fully he was distracted by his own thoughts and evaluating what was happening.

Cooper speaking to no one again responded, "I'm so thirsty." Then asked "Did anyone bring water?"

"Not me." Answered Will.

"Ya, me either." Said Henry.

Shadows appeared around every corner as exhaustion set in. With each new hill they climbed they hoped to see a road magically pop out of the underbrush, but with each new hill another hill or two popped out instead. With the snow on the ground, it began to get slippery and steep hills thick brush and deadfall made it extremely difficult to make good time, it was getting more clear by the second that they were not where they thought they were. Each boy took turns reading the compass to confirm and validate the direction they were headed, and each one fought back fear.

"I don't get it! Are we going the right way, or aren't we?" Henry spoke up.

"The compass said we are, and we can't see the sun....so...... who knows?" Will replied.

They were all getting cold, hungry, and thirsty. None of the trio were dressed for colder weather. Will had on an insulated rain jacket, jeans and tennis shoes, Henry had a thick hooded sweatshirt and light hiking boots. Cooper was dressed the best in a lightweight winter coat and some snow boots. However, in October in Alaska at night they would struggle to stay warm. The storm clouds loomed, signaling a change in weather. Unwilling to admit it, the realization crept in-they might be lost. The dense forest seemed to close in on them, but the boys pressed on, convinced they were walking east pushing through the underbrush the sticks and branches catching and scratching their clothes and faces but paying no attention they ran smack dab into a clearing, and they could see the edge of a very big lake. With the deepening snow, the darkening forest, and their exhausted dehydrated and hungry young bodies it might as well have been an ocean (Later they would learn it was Finger Lake).

Cooper yelled, “Where are we?” “This isn’t Mosquito Lake.”

“Holy *#@*,” Cooper said. Cooper let out a slurry of curse words that Will and Henry had never heard from him before. After the cursing, and exasperation, and futility of their situation had set in for what felt like 10 minutes, when in fact it was 10 seconds.

Henry interrupted the hallow silence, “We can’t get around this tonight, and this shouldn’t even be on our path.”

“We couldn’t get around this with a boat,” Cooper said. His head dropping as he half fell in the snow, his optimism and energy depleted.

“We aren't supposed to get around this. We didn’t pass this lake.” Will noted. “Hey, don’t you think my dad will be looking for us by now? Maybe, we should stay put and wait for help? Isn’t that what we’re told, stay put if you think your LOST.” Will did not want to stay put or say LOST outloud.

“But, that bear!” Cooper said just loud enough for the others to hear. Oh, God that bear he knew they were all thinking about it.

Henry spoke up, “Something is wrong with that compass and this stupid lake shouldn’t be here.” His voice gaining urgency and volume as he said it.

“What do you guys think we should do then?” Will said with more sarcasm than he meant.

Cooper could be heard saying under his breath, “I want to go home, and I want a drink of water and a hamburger.”

“We’re lost!” Henry said in no uncertain terms.

“No, the roads got to be close.” said Will, “We went straight East.”

“The road moved, you dummies.” Coop blurted out.

“Buck up Cooper. We are going to make a shelter, and start a fire, and we are going to eat these rabbits,” Henry said only half believeing that this was the right course of action, but having no idea at this point what the best course of action was.

Will in a decisive tone declared, “We are stopping for the night we have to prepare for a cold night, and we can’t wait until it gets darker to do it.” He did not want to say the word “LOST" again.

They couldn’t let the panic get to them the fear was shoved down. They had to keep it together and get out of here.

Henry agreed as he pushed fear down, "This clearing is as good a spot as any."

"Is everyone cold? I'm cold." Will announced. "We need to start a fire." "I have been cold since we started to head back, my feet are wet and frozen, my gloves are worthless, and my coat is losing insulation from the brush tearing it. I haven't felt my fingers for a while." He had brought regular tennis shoes which were ideal for hunting and chasing rabbits but the worst thing for what they were walking in now. His feet were wet, and his thin gloves that were good for handling a gun and a knife while hunting were not warm enough and now they were soaked through. The hard terrain had left it's mark on his coat. Hours of branches tearing at it and the snow soaking it made it look almost useless.

Cooper replied, "I'm not cold, I'm tired and hungry, and both my legs are cramping to the point I don't think I can go on right now." The cold had not completely set in on the trio because of the heavy hiking they had been doing.

Cooper was not keen on the idea of camping and asked, "Well what are we gonna do when it gets dark?"

Will replied "There is nothing out here after dark that isn't here right now!"

Henry added, "The only thing different after dark is no light source and it's going to get very cold, but a fire will take care of both, and you shouldn't have worn those concrete filled boots hunting," Henry chided him.

"Hey, at least I'm **not** cold," Cooper shot back at him again.

"It's definitely going to get cold tonight you guys, I think the temperature will drop 20 degrees," Henry said. His calculations seemed spot on for the area and the season, "we can't be wet and not have a shelter and fire if we are going to survive the night. What is it 10 degrees now? It will be below zero possibly tonight. If we don't find shelter and make a fire, we're going to be in trouble."

"I agree" Will stated. "Start grabbing firewood."

"I'm gonna just sit down for a second." Cooper whispered to himself.

So, once the decision was made, and the word **lost** had been spoken; they all took deep breaths, picked up their guns, and headed into the clearing. They assessed the small clearing and searched around for the best place to have a fire. On the edge of the clearing was an old tree that had been knocked over roots and all by the wind. A rootball is what they call it in Alaska when a tree falls with the all the roots still attached.

"Look at this tree it's great with this giant rootball!" said Henry as he quickly laid under the rootball portion of the fallen tree." Oh, man I could lay here a while." Henry educating them aloud "It's crazy that these trees fall with all their roots attached in a wet summer."

"Ya," said Coop "Some trees snap at the trunk and the roots stay frozen in the ground in the winter storms, but when they fall roots and all what a great windbreak for us hunters." He laughed. "Maybe I'll take a quick break under here too. We just need some grass for bedding to get off the dirt and wet ground." He jumped up and started ripping tall grass out and throwing it on the ground under the rootball for a makeshift bed.

"Your gonna need a lot of that." Will said, "and we are going to need a whole lot of wood and kindling."

As Will was looking around, he said "Isn't this an old burn area from a long time ago? I can see all the way around the clearing," Will continued. "This will be a good place to have a fire. We can see that bear coming from here too." and Will made a mental note to keep the gut pile of rabbits far from their camp. They got to work collecting grass and wood with the urgency in the back of their minds that their lives depended on it. But no one talked about their fears aloud.

The night had not yet begun, and they joked before, but none of them had said it with any true sincerity that it was now life and death. They weren't maybe lost, or kind of lost, but really lost and in a blizzard in Alaska with no idea which direction to go or what to do or most importantly how they got here.

Chapter Five

BEAVER FEVER

The trio spread out and gathered grass and wood and worked themselves towards Finger Lake which at the time they did not know. It was just a lake that wasn't supposed to be there to them.

"Dang," said Cooper "The lake is iced over, take a look at this you guys." Cooper hit the edge of the lake first and he hadn't moved that fast for an hour, but he was sooo thirsty.

"Guess, we're chopping this out," said Will

"Don't use your gun!" Henry snapped. "You have the slug for the bear we can't get that damaged and let's not unload it." Henry did not want to use his new gun as an axe and...as they were speaking Cooper emptied his .22 and hollered to them, "Use mine it will work the best for chopping and mine won't be used to kill the bear if we wreck it anyway." Cooper quickly approached the edge of the lake took the barrel and started a stabbing motion, bashing the ice over and over and over until there was a large enough access hole to get all three boys a drink. They dropped to their knees seeing the water and they drank like animals slurping with their hands to get enough to be satisfied. At some point, as they were all slurping Henry commented and advised as he drank

"There could be Beaver Fever bacteria in this lake. My dad's friend got it this fall hunting moose."

"What? In this lake?" Cooper said.

"I don't think so, but I know it can be anywhere in these woods with Beavers close by."

Yeah, some parasite called "guarded". Cooper interjected between slurping.

"NO" corrected Henry, "Giardia," is what it's scientific name is but everyone calls it Beaver Fever."

Henry kept explaining. "It's pure diarrhea for weeks and on top of that its greasy diarrhea and fever, my dad's friend was sick for weeks and he smelled bad. When he burped it was like he was rotten or swallowed something dead he smelled so bad."

They stopped drinking only momentarily to give a quick overview of the lake that they could only see part of. They weren't sure if they cared because thirst was overtaking them. Their hands were cold, and their knees were now wet and muddy, but they needed a drink of water **so** bad. None of the trio had ever experienced Beaver Fever but many hunters warned of the parasite and its wrath. Beaver Fever could last 2-6 weeks with a fever, diarrhea, nausea, vomiting, horrific gas and bloating but also greasy stools. They also understood now, being so thirsty, why you ignored the warnings and drank anyway.

“I guess I’ll take my chances, I don’t see any beaver huts.” Will said slurping still.

“Me too.” said Cooper

“Yea, I guess me too.” Henry agreed. "I can’t stop now.”

While Cooper took another quick breath he looked right and left on the shore and yelled excitedly to the others, “Cranberries! I found cranberries,” Cooper yelled excitedly.

“Oh my God I’m so hungry.” Will chimed in and jumped closer to Cooper and fell on his knees again where Cooper was pulling them from and joined him.

(In mid-October, most of the berries were gone or dried up, but the season had been warmer that year so some cranberries could still be picked.)

Will after grabbing what he could find of cranberries and cramming them in his mouth raced frantically around the part of the lake they were on to look for more berries.

“Rosehips!” Will yelled and grasped what handfuls he felt he could shove in his mouth and his pockets. All Will could think about was that they had to get that fire going before dark.

"I'll bring you guys some." Will shouted. He wasn't even sure they heard because their heads were down frantically looking for more cranberries.

"Hey, do your moms let you guys eat these rosehips off the wild rose bushes? I guess they have vitamin C and other good stuff or so my mom says. But their so sour and have so many seeds their hard to eat in handfuls."

Henry said, "I don't like them much, but my mom eats them here and there."

Cooper added, "My grandmother showed me when I was little the little bulb behind the dead rose petals. She told me the rosehip ate the petals and that's why the rose hip (the little bulb) behind the dead flower is so fat now and the rose is dead. Boy, did I believe that for a long time."

Will continued, "Another game we had was when my cousins were all there playing outside, we could see who could shove the most in their mouth. It would pucker you good and you had to chew and eat them and swallow them with all the seeds, no spitting them out to win. Boy, we loved eating stuff outside. Then your poop had all the rosehip seeds in it. Ha, Ha!"

Coop was scouring the ground again. "What are you doing now?" said Will.

"Well at soccer we would sit on the sidelines and eat chamomile heads off the little weed, and they were pretty good too, kind of lemony. I'm looking for some of those.

"Those are probably frozen and gone, Good Luck!" replied Will.

There were not enough berries to get full and darkness was coming fast. They didn't have time to keep searching the bushes for berries, so they headed back to the clearing.

The snow falling from the overcast sky offered no peace. After being somewhat satisfied with some water the boys worked quickly. Almost in a state of panic about being lost and being cold. Wood and grass was gathered swiftly. The frenzy to gather enough wood intensified. It was hard to gauge how much they would need or how fast and hot it would burn. If the wood was too wet, it would smolder and not put off enough heat.

Looking over his shoulder Will could see Cooper lifting his heavy boots through the snow as he gathered wood. A look of sternness and decisiveness about him. Then he saw Coopers shape collapse in the distance and he was just far enough away that he couldn't hear the painful noises coming from him. But the way he was rolling back and forth, he knew it was another leg cramp. Henry was close by and both boys hurried over to him.

"I can't believe none of us grabbed any water to bring?" said Henry.

"Yeah, what were we thinking?" said Will,

"We were thinking we were going to hunt for 2 hours and be leaving." said Cooper angry with himself.

"We may have to go back to the lake." announced Henry "and fill ourselves up before dark."

"We have to gut rabbits and still make a fire before dark." answered Will. "The snow is making the sky darker more quickly than usual with the cloud cover."

"Do you think we have enough wood yet?" Cooper asked. "I need to sit down for a minute."

"I don't know," Will replied. "But it will have to be, we need to start this fire before we lose what little light is left and I am getting so cold."

They knew they had limited time before it was completely dark, and it wasn't just preparing for the cold and dark. It would be a long night with freezing fingers, empty bellies and no sleep. But that would still only be a small portion of their long night of terror ahead.

Chapter Six

ONE MATCH FIRE CHALLENGE

At Will's house learning how to start a fire was essential. Will's mom was not good at starting a fire and they lived in a cabin with a wood stove as the primary source to keep their house warm. Will's dad, Patrick taught the kids the art of starting a fire methodically, emphasizing good fire-starting materials. The challenge involved using only one match to ignite a carefully arranged pile of dry tinder and kindling. Blowing air strategically was crucial to keep the fire alive and growing. His mom grew up in the city and was not at all patient with the fire process. A "one match fire" became the traditional game challenge of anyone who was at their house frequently, including girls. His sisters were both particularly good at the "One Match Fire Challenge."

Will began, "Ok, you two have both been at my house when my dad made us try the 1 match fire challenge, so we all need to find dry tinder and limbs for kindling. Remember

look under a spruce tree even with this snow to find something dry enough to start a fire tonight. And we have to hurry. It's getting dark."

"Oh, I remember," said Coop, "Your dad told me to get "Moose Beard" off the trees and use it for tinder and I had no idea what he was talking about, I thought he was tricking me again like when he talked about the board stretcher." Cooper continued, "And he makes you nervous just watching. He said he wasn't timing us but then he knew how long it took us to get that fire going." Cooper was spreading out to grab his own tinder for his own 1 match fire pile.

"I remember when you had your fire prepped and ready to light you would tell him and then the challenge would begin. Plus, he would question you on where you got your tinder and kindling if he wasn't watching you." Henry added. "I agree with Coop, he said you weren't timed, and it was all about just getting the fire started with 1 match, but I swear he was timing us."

"Ya, he probably was, I knew right where to get the dry Moose Beard off our trees in our yard for the tinder portion of the fire or grab wood shavings from the garage instead of shave them with my pocketknife if my dad wasn't watching and kindling sticks were everywhere in our yard." Will explained. "But, he had us do it a lot, so we got fast at it. If we got pretty good at the challenge, he would wait until it was raining and then have one of us do it. Yikes, that got tricky."

The trio quickly grabbed handfuls of tinder from under the spruce boughs and moose beard moss off trunks and brought it close to the rootball shelter to make their own fire start pile. They continued to scour the surroundings searching for dry tinder to ignite the core of the fire until Cooper hollered, he was ready.

Cooper hollered out and tried his fire first, "I am going to make some shavings with my pocketknife and this birch sapling for tinder for the fire. I am sure you two don't know this trick." Cooper laughed.

Henry challenged, "I will prepare a tee pee which is a popular method." But, before Henry lit the first match, Will said, "Stop, we need a quick inventory of our matches. How many matches do we have?

"Oh, good idea," Henry pulled out his matches and started counting them. "I have a full book of 24 matches here."

Cooper pulled his packet out, "I have 7 matches."

Will pulled his packet of matches out and to his surprise there were only 2 matches. He grabbed the wrong packet of matches his book of matches was almost used up.

"We should have plenty of matches, we should be fine," Cooper said, "let's get this fire going."

Henry took a deep breath, "Ok, here goes," and he struck a match. Nothing happened. He quickly struck the match again. Nothing. "What is the matter with these matches"? He grabbed another but to no avail.

"Wait, wait, wait, we can't afford to lose or waste matches." Coop yelled.

Cooper walked over and grabbed his book of matches from Henry. "These are damp Henry. Where did you have them stored"?

"In my front pocket, next to my Charleston Chew," he said.

Will interrupted, "Let me see those matches." After inspecting them he stated. "Yea, Henry these are damp from your sweat and walking all day. These are worthless."

Cooper walked up and knelt near the place designated for the fire where he had started his shavings. "I've got this you guys, I got this. I am an Native Alaskan after all, and we thrive under pressure in the wilderness." He giggled.

"I hope you're right, Cooper" Will said honestly. Cooper stuck his feather stick and wood shavings into the ground and grabbed some dry grass and piled it around it's base. He lit his match, and everyone's eyes lit up as it struck true and a small orangish blue flame lit up. Everyone's mood was momentarily elevated. He applied the small flame to the grass, and it started to catch. First smoke, then a little more, and then a gust of wind came through and it was gone. Cooper tried again, and again. He was down to his last match. He struck it, and a flame caught some grass, which started to burn into the feather stick. It was working! He grabbed some of his tinder and applied just a little bit more of what he thought was dry grass and tinder. It immediately started smoking more.

"It's too wet Cooper, that much smoke isn't good," Will said.

"Smoke is always good with fire, Will, don't you know anything?" Cooper countered, glancing up and smiling at him. Will thought a second and nodded his head. "Ya, OK." Will handed Cooper some dry tinder that he had collected, and he and Henry stood with their backs to the wind, and arched their boyish frames into as big of wind blocks as they could muster. Covering the small flame from any large snowflakes or gusts of wind. More smoke, and more smoke, and then the fire disappeared, smothered.

Cooper didn't want to try any more. "I can't take this, it's your turn Will I am going to gut and strip a rabbit besides you've been fire trained." and Henry agreed with him, they both backed away and started grabbing the rabbits from the Minnie Mouse backpack.

Henry and Cooper engaged in a debate now about the best method for stripping and gutting the animals. They tried to distract themselves from what Will was doing. It was Will's turn to try to get the fire started. Will's hands were shaking from the cold, or from the nerves. A shaky hand with an important match could be it – they would freeze to death. Shaking a match can put it out, you can drop it or apply it incorrectly. He was cold but he had been preparing for this moment since he could remember with his father. I can do it, he thought.

He had never slept outside in the snow without a tent, much less without a fire; and he had spent his whole life in Alaska. Will was patient and methodical, calming himself with deep breaths. He thought to himself, so when I do this the best is when my father is watching me. He imagined his father coaching him through the preparation like he was looking over his shoulder talking him through every step. "You want the dryest tinder you can find. Don't just find dry tinder at the base of the tree, dig underneath that dry tinder and find even drier tinder and kindling." Then he imagined trying to start the fire and saw in his mind's eye wind and snow blowing the fire out. He heard his father tell him, "You need a good wind block and if it is raining you have to have something protecting your tinder and your match." So he moved it under the spruce tree closer to the rootball shelter. Then he thought back to his father doing this himself while camping. He would make a pile of small sticks, slightly bigger sticks and so on in three piles – all small but different variants. "You are picking which sticks to put on and their order, you have to be precise." His fathers voice echoed in his head.

He uncovered his matches and removed them from his pocket. One thing he had remembered to do even though he forgot his lighter, was to wrap the matches in a something waterproof.

He glanced back at Henry who was carving up the rabbits.

"We gotta get those guts and skins away from our camp." Will yelled towards them.

"Ya, I have the guts and skins on this long grass to carry it away." Henry responded.

Cooper was adding to their shelter. Both had seen it fit to quit stacking firewood and work on food and shelter. Before he looked back to the task at hand, he pictured how much his family meant to him and how much Henry and Cooper meant to him, and he said a silent prayer, "Lord please make sure my friends are taken care of no matter what happens. Amen."

He checked on his last two matches frustrated at himself again for grabbing the wrong matches and forgetting the lighter. He examined them closely and saw that one had a head that was damaged and falling off. He wasn't even sure it would strike without falling off let alone setting fire to something. So, he doubled down and decided to add this match to the bottom of his dry tinder pile to help it get started. This meant that Will was down to his last match. He was living out his father's game, the one match challenge. It was cold, with blizzard conditions with big wet snowflakes flying in from the side hitting his face. His hands were shaking, and if felt like their lives hung in the balance.

The one match challenge was now, he was living it. Only this time it was for real, not a game, but a life and death situation. For the first time Will understood why his father had made him and his sisters learn about starting a campfire; and why his father had them try the one match challenge on rainy days. Will took a deep breath and struck his final match. Then softly but decisively placed it in the center of his tinder pile. Again, adding perfectly placed perfectly chosen slivers of wood one at a time from his three piles. The flame grew and grew and in a few minutes his shoulders finally slumped back, and relaxed as he added some more sticks to the fire. He knew this fire would survive snow and now so would they.

"You got that fire yet?" Coop hollered, "I got a skinny rabbit ready to roast ha ha!"

"Just about got it." Will responded relieved watching the fire grow until it was ready to burn alone. Henry and Cooper had prepared the rabbits, and they were now breaking off spruce boughs and braiding them in and out of branches they had placed on the sides of each of the rootballs side walls.

It was now a three-sided wind block, and even had about a two-foot overhang of protection from the snow.

"Henry that's amazing," Will exclaimed, "those rabbits look to die for." Henry turned around and saw the beautiful fire Will had started.

"Ha, to die for, very funny!" Henry replied.

"Thank God it started, you did it," he said the relief apparent in the tone of his voice. They glanced behind them, and Cooper was howling, "Ooow-woo, ooowwooo," doing a dance around the fire like a good omen. Henry and Will joined in.

"Here's a rabbit stick for you too Will, ready to roast." Said Henry.

Will took the rabbit happily, "So, we have stick skewered rabbit roasted supper, too bad we don't have marshmallows to put on these sticks too!" Will commented.

They were not out of it yet, but they found themselves full of confidence for the next hour or so. Smiles for a naive hour before the coldness of the night really set in and the realization they would have no hamburgers tonight. But they were all grateful they had something to eat.

The boys skewered the rabbits like marshmallows after being cleaned as best they could, and the rabbits cooked slower than expected. As they devoured the meat, they discovered unwelcome pieces of broken bones and BBs peppered throughout the rabbit meat. They began spitting them out like it was a natural occurrence. The outside of the rabbit was burnt, and the inside was raw. They ate a layer of meat and returned it to the fire to cook. They continued until some of their hunger diminished.

"So much for a quick rabbit hunting trip." Henry began as they sat by the fire cooking rabbits.

"Yea, if we knew we were going to camp I would have brought a sleeping bag for sure." Coop added.

"If I would have known I would have brought some peanut butter and jelly sandwiches." Will said.

"When we get out of here, I want a Charleston Chew and 3 Big Mac's." added Henry.

Will giggled a little under his breath, but at the same time felt bad now because it was Will who picked up the partially eaten Charleston chew and ate it before they were lost and had nothing else to eat. He would tell Henry when all of this was behind them, he thought.

Cooper asked, "You think this rabbit will cook better spinning over the fire or shoved into the fire directly while charring the skin and giving it a well-done recipe?"

Will reported back "I am going for charred well done I want to eat it now!"

Henry thoughtfully replied, "I am twirling, roasting and taste testing until I like it."

Cooper again to no one in particular spoke out "I need salt, and I need another drink of water."

They did not want to travel back to the lake, the sky was now dark but there was no other water source, so they resorted to eating snow. The snow was delicious, and depending on where you grabbed a handful it could taste like a mild dirt flavor or a bit like spruce, but it was never quite satisfying enough after hiking for hours.

Henry spoke up first, "How are we going to handle water? We can't go another day of hiking without getting all of us some hydration. Cooper is cramping alot."

"Doesn't that make hypothermia worse?" Coop asked.

"Eating snow will lower your body temperature and it could make things worse. Maybe they really will find all of us out here huddled naked together." Will added. "Trying to get warm because we are ALL HYPOTHERMIC by the time we get found!" Another round of laughter echoed through the forest.

Cooper added, "I have been doing better the snow is helping. I just needed to rest, that's all – I'm fine. It's these boots being big and heavy."

"Well how cold are your feet," Will asked, "They are toasty," he laughed. "I feel bad, I was fairly warm all day."

"What?" the other two instantly and simultaneously replied? "How can you be warm? We are in a blizzard in Alaska at night"!

"Ha, yea that's true. Could it be my Native Alaskan blood"? He laughed again, "seriously though I have thick gloves, thick boots, a thick coat and a nice hat. What did you think we were doing out here? I mean look at Will, he has tennis shoes on, a coat that is leaking insulation, and thin cheap gloves on. I am worried about him, not me. Will where are your thin little gloves"?

"They are right there," he pointed at the edge of the fire where the gloves were placed on a log drying. "Oh no, just as he pointed at the gloves as if by some evil magic trick, they burst into flames. "Noooo!"

Will yelled and jumped over the fire and stomped on the glove putting it out. He held it up in the fire light. All four fingers had been burnt off. It was a problem but not much worse than he was with the gloves. "Shoot, we can't afford any more mistakes, let's do an inventory of gear, and go over things we should be thinking about." said Henry.

"How are yours Will?" Cooper asked.

"My what?"

"Your hands and feet, are they still cold?" Cooper asked genuinely concerned.

Will thoughtfully answered, "Well, I haven't felt them until the fire started and now they hurt." He said shaking them. "They throb like I can feel my heart pumping in them."

Henry was in a similar situation with his feet and added in, "If we can get our feet warm and somewhat dry tonight, then we might move more quickly tomorrow."

"How do we do that?" Will asked, when Henry chimed in "I am going to dry my shoes over the fire."

He attempted to take the first one off and hang it over the fire on a stick. But the stick immediately started bending into the center of the fire, and the trio dove for the shoe.

"That isn't going to work, plus we can't keep our feet warm tonight if we take our shoes off" Will reasoned.

"I think maybe the best thing we could do is stand as close to the fire as we possibly can without burning ourselves to dry our shoes out," Will continued.

Henry nodded and both boys inched closer and closer to the flames, and then they had to stop and back up, both coughing from the smoke. "Well, maybe not that close." Henry laughed.

It wasn't guaranteed they would get out of this mess ok or even alive, but if they made the right decisions and stuck together, they could do this. "My gosh, what an adventure we are on," Will spoke out.

Will's father often spoke about adventures and hard things in life, about growing up and being a man, or just an adult. It was hard he would say and often explained to Will, and even Henry and Cooper on occasion. Will added "I can hear my dad tell us, the hardest things in your life are the most worthwhile. They help you grow and become the best version of yourself. You will never know if you aren't tested and it is almost impossible to test yourself, life has to do it and will do it for you." Plus, he would always add, "the best stories and the best times of your life will not be fun while you are in the story, in the moment and during the adventure, it's after the adventure when you remember it and reminisce with important people that you will truly understand the full impact of an adventure, how it bonds you to people for the rest of your life." Will was beginning to understand this oh too well. The trio was thoughtfully silenced for a split second.

"Ya, an adventure alright" said Coop "We are no Swiss Family Robinson."

"Ya, or Jeremiah Johnson" Henry added. They all laughed. The so-called adventure was just getting started.

Chapter Seven

GUNSHOTS

After eating rabbits Will gathered the compass in hand and the trio tried to reevaluate what happened and where to being tomorrow. “How did this happen we were watching this compass and ended up here. Wherever "here" is." Will spewed frustratedly.

"It's definitely a mystery." Answered Henry. "Did we veer too far out from the bear tracks?"

"It doesn't seem like it, the compass still showed us going east all day." Will said.

"Now which way do we start in the morning?" Cooper questioned.

"Well, we have to keep the fire going all night, it has to be attended and we cannot under any circumstances let it go out!" Will informed the group changing the subject for a minute.

Cooper begged, "Can I please lay down first, I gotta lay down."

"Sure" said Henry and replied, "This will be like the movies, and we do it in shifts, keep the bear gun close and loaded and keep the fire up. You have to watch the outer ring for the bear and listen for him."

"Right!" said Will, "The wood is wet, and some is rotten, and the snow is not helping, so when it's your turn you have to really watch and keep it stoked, it's gonna be smokey probably no matter what, just don't let it go out!"

"Got it!" said Coop

"Yep" said Henry

The one keeping watch over the fire, would stand and scan the outer ring of the clearing for sign of that monster bear they had followed all day or that followed them. The boys would not leave the fire, because at this point, they could all sense and feel that without it they would not survive.

Will added "To seal the agreement, put your hands in the center like a pact, so that if the bear attacks nobody runs. We face the bear as a team."

Coopers' hands went in and so did Henry's. They went down and lifted their hands out of the circle of the pact, and each replied differently.

"Fire!" said Will

"Bear!" said Cooper.

"Team," said Henry. None of them realizing until then what they were all really thinking.

Will was amazed that this act of comradery and placing their hands in as a sign of unity gave him confidence and made him feel better. Sure, he was still scared to death, but in those situations when life is on the line, just a small little comfort like knowing your two best friends were next to you and you were going to get through this together. It made him feel like they were in a war, and it was going to be a battle, a battle for their survival and they would defend each other. This was a worthy adventure, just not one they would have dreamed of.

The night crept in, and the fire while warm only kept half your body warm. The half on the fire's side was warm and the other half frozen. It wasn't just that they were tired and cold – exhausted really – they were miserable even with the fire. The miserable situation of the night set in affecting their thoughts and attitudes.

"You guys tell me what you decide about which direction to go tomorrow. I am laying down." Cooper announced. "Besides I can hear you over here."

While continuing to discuss plans they heard gunshots ever so faintly. The boys went silent for a moment and then perked right up.

Henry intently said, "Did you guys hear that?"

"Ya," said Will, "Barely can hear it."

"Are they guns? Its little pops!" said Coop

"Shhhhh," said Will "listen again."

"It's rifles." Said Henry

"Where are they? 100 miles away? Are they for us?" asked Cooper

"We're saved!" Cooper bellowed.

"Seems like it," said Henry, "Why else would someone be shooting in the dark?"

"Where are they coming from?" Henry listened intently. The gunshots were so far away and were they really for them?

"Why are they so far away; how can that be? They aren't coming from the same place." Will added. "That's confusing."

The boys were lost, and these shots were confusing because it seemed like they came from every direction. Firing gunshots in rounds of three was what the boys were hoping for because it was the sign of a location. People looking for you would try and give you their location so you could find your way to them. By shooting off three rounds, spaced a few seconds apart you were getting a specific message. The idea is you hear the first two shots and then you're listening very intently, so the third shot you can take a reading on a landmark and start walking towards it.

It sounded like some gunshots were one hill over. Then the next shot seemed so far away they barely could hear it. (For hours the boys were hearing shots that were coming from different directions because rescuers were traveling way north on Swanson River

Rd and then south on the road hoping for return fire from the boys not realizing the different directions were very confusing for them.)

Cooper relaxed into a deep breath.

"Coop those gunshots could be ten miles away depending on lots of different factors." Henry further explained to Cooper, "We still can't figure out which way to head out in the morning with the shots in all directions?"

"Shouldn't we fire back?" Cooper questioned.

"We don't have very many bullets left." Said Will "We should wait and see if we are going to need them or if they will get easier to figure out where they are coming from."

It didn't give them a bit of comfort knowing that the rescue team was sending them such mixed signals.

"We can't go find them or walk through the dark without injuring ourselves tripping out of here with no flashlight and get more lost tonight, if that's even possible. So, let's hope they are still shooting them off in the morning," Will assessed out loud.

Henry wasn't satisfied, "I know every time we hear a gunshot it's in a different direction, so how do we decide which gunshots to walk towards"?

"It sounds like we could walk one direction and find them by tomorrow," Cooper confidently spoke from underneath his grassy bed. Henry walked towards him stomping out the grass next to the fire every few minutes as it caught on fire and traced its way towards Cooper and their shelter.

"I don't think that will work, Coop" Henry paused, "you can hear gunshots for 20 miles in the right places, and the sounds can bounce off different lakes, hills, mountains, you name it. We could walk the wrong direction easily and end up out here another night without a fire. Those gunshots are all over the place, totally mixed signals."

"Is that why we are hearing them all around us, the search party is just confusing us. Come this way, no not that way over here, turn around and come this way." Cooper laughed at his joke, but it was a good point. How did they expect us to pick a direction when the gunshots were coming from so many directions? Or was that just the hills bouncing sound around? They had no clue.

"I got it! I'm a genius," Henry enthusiastically stated, "I've got it, this is the only way we can do this unless we hear something more clear and more definitive," he paused, "we must track the noises using statistics," "We will mark with sticks the direction of the shot every time we hear them, then in the morning when it is time to go, the direction with the most sticks or rather gunshots wins, and we walk that way."

"It's not perfect, but it could work." said Will thinking about it a little longer. They would fight a bear together, cuddle to stay warm at night together, and walk in whatever direction most of the gunshots came from – yes, together. Poetic if not youthfully naive. What better option did they have?

After they listened to the gunshots for a time, they finally started to take turns laying down……

As far as sleeping in a blizzard Cooper was the only one who got good sleep, in his warm gear, but only for an hour or so a few times. Will and Henry woke him after about 45 minutes because he was not moving and with three layers of grass on top of him and an inch and a half of snow piled on top of the silhouette of his body, it made for an eerie site. Cooper looked as if he had passed away in the night. He was deathly still. Both Henry and Will looked at each other concerned.

Henry said quietly, "Cooper."

"Cooper," Will loudly exclaimed. "Cooper," even louder this time. And then both boys together, "Cooper!" They shook him awake.

"WHHAAATTT?" he was annoyed and understandably so. It would have been nice to get some sleep. "Geez you guys, leave me alone."

"My god we thought you were dead," Henry explained. "You weren't moving or breathing."

"You were just jealous that I am warm and able to sleep. Ha! serves me right I suppose I do have all the warm gear.

Henry left his shift to Will and went and piled grass in the shelter on top of himself. This left Will standing alone at the fire during his shift, he figured around 1 a.m. Cooper may have been sleeping but he couldn't tell, Will could tell Henry was huddled up next to Cooper for warmth because every so often the two would giggle and Cooper would say, "get off of me," to which Henry retorted with, "but I'm cold Cooper." Eventually the two wiggled close enough to each other to spoon. It was something he would tease them about later, but not now, because it was life and death now and they needed to be warm he filed the memory away for use later for teasing after they got themselves out of this little predicament.

Chapter Eight

ON THE OTHER SIDE

That fateful night on the other side to the east of where the boys were on Swanson River Road right next to Mosquito Lake and at the sign where the truck was parked, Patrick was trying to determine exactly what went wrong and why the boys had never appeared at the meeting sign. He had driven up and down the road thinking they just came out at a different spot. But there was not a trace of them to be found. As he drove up and down the road he was honking and hollering for a long time. He finally had to start calling home and to his brother's house to see if someone by some chance had picked them up and he was not notified. Cell service was bad in this area. No one he called had seen them so now he was pushing down panic and thoughts of the worst.

It was discovered around 2:00 pm that the boys were not at each other's homes. Patrick called his brother Mark who had four boys of his own, Will's cousins who lived on the Kasilof River. The boys could fish for world-famous salmon right outside their house on the river and Mark owned boats that the boys could use. It was a young man's paradise. Brown bears would frequent that area of the Kasilof River and again the boys were alert to the fact that they could appear anytime near that river looking for a world class fish dinner too, but as stated before it was part of their everyday life.

After the phone call to locate the trio Mark left for Swanson River Road knowing immediately something had gone wrong. Mark knew Alaska. He also knew that between the landscape, the guns, winter settling in, and 3 boys there were more bad scenarios than he could bear to think about. Mark grabbed bear guns and survival supplies.

In the meantime, Junie, Will's mom, had also been trying to call the one cell phone that she thought Will had on him. But there was absolutely no cell service in the Swanson River Road Area, which was a problem the whole time.

Mark met Patrick on Swanson River Road and with a backpack and bear guns the men prepared for a search and rescue of their own. If bears were out and not hibernating yet they would either be hungry and/or angry. The State troopers arrived and tried to stop all rescue plans of hiking at night. They did not know the determination or the experience of the two men they were talking to.

Once the phone calls were done Junie got in the car and took off to the Swanson River Road area. The Hills and the Bakers, both parents of both families, arrived shortly thereafter.

Decisions were made quickly about what to do now that it was getting dark, and It had started to snow, which would add further complications. The tracks that Patrick and Mark hoped to follow would be lost under the snow. More people arrived to offer help. The troopers been driving up and down Swanson River Road with sirens blaring and firing shots in the air, hoping to give direction to the boys but they drove miles down the road to the north and miles to the south firing shots not realizing they created confusion for the boys who were hearing the shots from what felt like all over the forest. Patrick and Mark were also shooting rifles off hoping the boys would repeat the fire to give direction as to their whereabouts. It was a very, very, very long night. Most of the parents were on the phone to someone for either rescue help or with concerned family and friends.

Mark stayed on the phone throughout the night along with Charles who was Henry's dad. Mark and Charles had gone to school together in their youth. They were trying to get any plane in the area to go up and search at first light. Mark had been in Alaska for 35 years and knew everyone. Mark, glued to the phone, continued his relentless pursuit of a plane willing to brave the weather and assist in the search. Every rejection, every voice on the other end explaining the impossibility due to the weather, heightened the tension. The clock ticked away; each moment felt like an eternity.

Both men were looking for methods of rescue. It was nightfall and it was snowing. Even the Civil Air Patrol in the area would not fly up due to the weather conditions. As the search plans continued, the cold reality set in—the blizzard was diminishing the chances of finding any trace of the boys. The initial optimism of the search party began to wane, replaced by a somber acknowledgment of the challenges ahead. Family members, friends, and concerned locals gathered, exchanging worried glances and whispered words of encouragement. Parents and family clung to the hope of any updates, their eyes flickering watching the surrounding forest as if willing the boys to emerge. Night had fallen and planes were no longer an option until daybreak.

By the next morning Mark, Charles, Bob and Patrick after having explored alternative rescue methods decided to hike in themselves. A group of horses and riders gathered to go in on horseback to look for the boys. All the efforts to get a bush pilot failed due to the weather conditions even the next morning. All the pilots said there was no visibility, and it was too dangerous. They had to wait for the weather to clear. Well, the longer they waited the higher the chance that somebody might not make it out alive. Everyone was bustling around trying not to show visible signs of panic. Thoughts were going through their heads that perhaps the boys didn't make it out because of a gun accident, a bear problem, a different injury, and what if they had got separated? Suppressing those thoughts was extremely hard to do.

People kept arriving throughout the next morning. Even an ambulance appeared to await news or the arrival of the trio. All of Will's uncles were now there. Mark, Matt, and Michael along with their spouses who joined the collective effort. Zach, Will's older cousin, also appeared to bolster the rescue effort. The collective spirit remained resilient, with food and drinks provided by family and friends to sustain those involved. The Civil Air Patrol was called one last time in the morning and the patrol explained they were still grounded due to unfavorable weather conditions.

So, just at dawn, battling the elements, Patrick, Bob, and Zach embarked on a rescue trek into the challenging terrain, armed with bear guns and supplies. They were determined to navigate the wilderness and bring the boys back to safety. They faced their own set of obstacles, maneuvering through the dense vegetation and treacherous terrain with no tracks to follow.

Mark and Charles stayed back to coordinate the rescue. Troopers kept trying to shut down the efforts and did not put forth ideas other than firing shots into the air from the road. As for the group of rescue horses, they were waiting for one more person before they began their trek in. A professional rescue hiking group started their hike into the woods that morning and they quickly got turned around and ended up back on the road from which they started within an hour. They had also gotten turned around in the thick brush and forest. It was quite unnerving for those who did not know the wilderness and were hopeful others did. They had to reevaluate their strategy before beginning again. The collective hope that had fueled the previous night's efforts and ideas now contended with the harsh truth of the Alaskan wilderness and its ever-challenging, never-ending obstacles. Fear and disappointment loomed.

Chapter Nine

WOLF SIGHTING

As darkness continued to surround them like a fatal story the boys could still hear gunshots ever so faintly in the distance. Will sitting by the fire alone on watch questioned to himself, why were they so far away? Well at least someone knew they were lost and that was a relief. But were those shots coming from Swanson River Road? Will knew he could hear a gun range 8 miles from his home on a summer evening outside better than he could hear these gunshots. That was very disturbing. It seemed as if they must have been coming from somewhere else. Another hunter? Perhaps a gun range near the town of Sterling that Will did not know about? It was puzzling. Will thought they should have been much closer to the road. But as time went on it became obvious that the shots were for them because they continued throughout the night. Initially, the trio thought that they would walk out in the dark if the gunshots were close. But that was not the case. Sirens were also going off along with honking car horns, but the boys never heard the horns that night because they were so far away. The boys had been walking the opposite way to safety because of the broken compass which they had not yet accepted.

As temperatures dropped, the snowfall was relentless. Fatigue and anxiety took its toll on the boys as they rotated between fitful attempts at rest and vigilant wakefulness. Each passing hour deepened the uncertainty of their situation. After the initial gunshots and the fact that they were going in the wrong direction, they all listened for the gunshots during their turn on fire watch to see if an accurate direction from which they could work towards could be solidified.

The boys had also taken turns lying down on the grass that they gathered under the rootball so that they were not lying on the wet, cold ground. They felt extremely tired, but, between anxiety and the cold and hunger, none of them could stay asleep long. Hours after the gunshots had started and continued Cooper got up and walked outside the small campfire area to go pee. Seconds later, Cooper jumped back into the camp area in the safety of the fire. He was pointing and half screaming, he saw eyes and heard a noise just past the fire but couldn't see what it was.

"Oh, @! #*!,Theres something out there. Right there, geez, I saw eyes and they were moving towards me. Oh My God!" Cooper was screaming franticly!

"What is it?" Will said.

"I don't know, I could only see his eyes! Oh My God!" Cooper was shaking his hands and jumping a bit going towards his gun to pick it up and point it into the darkness.

Henry was now frightened awake and standing next to the others having grabbed his gun and pointed it into the darkness as well.

"Where is it?" Henry yelled back. "What is it? Anyone?"

Will had been on watch again for the second time and had not seen or heard anything but now he jumped up from the fire with the bear gun in hand and all the boys searched and scanned, right, left, right, left, to see if they could spot what Cooper though he saw.

"Was it the bear Coop?" Will spit out.

"I'm freaking out!" yelled Coop "I don't know what it was, it had scary eyes!"

The first thing on everybody's mind was, did Cooper possibly see a bear? Was that bear following them because of the bloody rabbit backpack? Or were they in his domain? Or possibly the gunfire had pushed whatever animal it was towards them. Was that animal now agitated?

The boys became quiet. Will made a quick cry out, "Watch where you point those guns. Don't just shoot, it could be a person, DO NOT PANIC."

Cooper said, "If it was a person, they would have announced themselves. These were not the eyes of a person," Cooper yelled.

The boys were still searching in the darkness and suddenly, Henry saw it, it was a wolf.

"There it is! IT'S A WOLF!" he yelled, and He lifted his gun and pointed it toward the wolf. "It's a wolf, Cooper is that what you saw?" Henry still half yelling.

Will screamed, "Don't shoot yet, just watch it." Will and Henry were now parallel to each other. And Cooper was still scanning to see if they could see more.

"I guess that's what I saw, I don't know. Are there more? Are we being circled?" Coop lashed out.

"I don't know either I can't see." Henry screamed back.

Was it going to come closer to the fire? Cooper also stoked the fire hoping to make it bigger and more forbidding to the wolf. The wolf made a terribly slow forward appearance. He held steady. All eyes were on him.

"Watch your gun!" screamed Henry yelling at both boys as they were all pivoting with guns at hand. None of them sure which way was safe from a predator.

"I can't tell what's happening, I can't see anything," screamed Will. "There could be a pack with him."

"He's coming in." announced Henry.

Guns were raised. The boys' eyes were scanning, scanning, scanning to see if there were more eyes, more wolves.

"Not yet," said Will "Don't shoot just yet, watch him, watch him."

Will knew there could be more in the background. And if they shot one wolf the other wolves, if they were out there, would come forward and possibly eat their wolf mate and coming forward would mean coming closer to the boys.

A year ago, his dog Gus, a large Boston terrier was almost eaten by wolves. A wolf came into the yard timidly. Will watched as the scene unfolded. Gus raced towards it aggressively barking. The wolf tucked its tail as if to leave and as it went into the woods, Gus followed thinking he had him on the run. However, four wolves appeared and started creeping closer. They were going to attack Gus. It was like gangsters. In an instant, his mother had seen this going down and was already running outside screaming, yelling, and throwing her arms around as fast as she could towards the wolves in the woods. The wolves became alarmed and took off back into the woods. She pulled Gus into the house slammed the door and sighed with relief astonished at the event.

Will knew plenty of wolf stories. He had heard many living in Alaska and was aware you could not trust what you could see.

"OK, I'm gonna fire a shot up and see if it scares it away." Will announced. "And maybe alert the rescue group where we are at the same time."

"Good idea," said Coop

"NO! you have the slug." Henry reminded him. "I got it this time." Henry shot into the air.

In just a split-second Coop reported nervously, "I can't see him anymore he backed away."

"Do you think those rescuers gunshots pushed the wolf at us?" Henry asked.

"Do you think there are more?" Coop questioned. "And what about that bear? Do you think those other gunshots will push the bear towards us?"

"I don't know" answered Will. "Whoever is shooting hopefully should hear our fire and assume it's us."

"Ya," said Will "or he's circling us and smelling rabbits, keep looking."

The trio had naturally backed themselves into each other forming a half circle to watch in all directions and see if the wolf would resurface somewhere else.

"Maybe he found the gut pile." Said Coop

"Maybe" said Henry.

"That was a wolf." stated Will. "It was way too big to be a coyote, big head and muzzle on him and big! Did he look big to you guys?"

"Definitely not a coyote. Coyotes are so small and skinny" agreed Henry. "You're lucky he didn't eat you why you were peeing Cooper."

"He was watching me that's for sure. I didn't even get to pee. I think I saw him at the same time he saw me." Cooper recounted. "Otherwise, don't you think he would have tried to jump me? But I jumped back to the fire before he could?"

"Could have been a lot of things." Henry said.

"Great, now we have to watch for wolves or one dumb lone wolf. We don't even know because we can't see. He or they may be waiting for one of us to be dumb enough to step outside the fire circle again." expressed Will.

"For all we know he was gonna eat us and the bloody rabbit gut pile if he did find it, the pile was the appetizer, and we were gonna be the real dinner." Coop said

"Ya, because wolves would eat boys and bloody rabbits, but maybe coyotes wouldn't try. Coyotes don't seem like they would be as aggressive with the fire." Henry added.

Hearing wolves howl when you were at home in your bed is one thing but to be five yards from them and looking them in the eye was another.

As the boys maintained their vigilance through the night, the chilling memory of the wolf encounter and the earlier sighting of brown bear paws and scat haunted their thoughts. The distant echoes of gunshots offered a strange comfort amidst the wilderness and the unseen threats that lurked in the shadows. The trio sat in silence, contemplating the whereabouts and concerns of their families.

"Do you think those gunshots are our parents?" Henry said worriedly.

“I think so,” said Will “My dad is probably losing his mind right now.”

“My mom will be so worried.” Added Cooper “She’s gonna kill me when this is over.”

They all laughed

“Ya me too,” said Will “Think we will make it to class on Monday?”

“Geez, Will I don’t want to spend another night out here, don’t even say that.” Henry barked.

“I can’t go back to sleep,” declared Coop, “STUPID WOLF!”

“Me too” agreed Henry “Feels like I can’t take my eyes off the perimeter.”

The trio stayed awake for some time, and the noises and shadows played tricks on their minds. Each rustle in the underbrush, every distant noise fueled their fears. The wilderness was indifferent to their plight. The wilderness now felt like a mortal enemy not a place of fun-filled adventure. It was a grueling long night watching for that wolf and of course, that brown bear was out there too somewhere.

As they laid in wait for another possible encounter, they stayed within the protective circle of the fire. The snow provided a source of hydration within arm's reach, and facing the darkness to relieve themselves within the light of the fire circle became a cautious ritual. The lost trio huddled around the once comforting glow of the campfire, wary of unseen eyes in the darkness but now it seemed feeble against the vastness of the wilderness. Before Will knew it, he had melted his tennis shoes and burnt and blistered his toes standing too close to the fire.

Will's feet were finally warm, not hot, just warm and then he noticed a sharp pain in them. "Ouch, that really hurt" he said. He looked down closer. As Will glanced down at his Nike tennis shoes, he noticed the front Nike sign was orange, and black not white, and that the front inch of his rubber sole had melted back into his shoe. He peeled off the shoes and examined his pruned, wet and cold feet. The front of every other toe on both feet were blistered, not blisters from the miles and miles they had trekked but blistered from the heat and melting rubber of his shoes. "How could I have not noticed," he thought perplexed. His feet were barely warm at this point. He started to worry, his feet must have been so cold for so long that he was losing sensation, or in other words frost bite was setting in. He rubbed his hands together pinching the tips of his fingers. Yup, he was losing sensation in the tips and outside area around his fingers on his right hand. The hand that he couldn't keep warm because he was carrying his gun with it. The hand that had the fingers on the gloves burnt just hours before. Yea, that hand. It made sense, he worried about it briefly, but it was really not painful, and he had bigger problems on his mind.

He was blessed in a way. "Funny," he thought it took getting lost in an Alaskan Blizzard for him to truly feel how blessed he was for everything, and everyone in his life. Make no mistake about it he was scared to death and would fight off tears and panic multiple times more throughout this ordeal if he was to get out of it at all, but he smiled genuinely so, and was truly grateful.

"Well, at least it seems like the gunshots are in one direction now, not 8." Said Henry.

"Some of the rescue teams are sleeping, unlike us or gave up!" Coop replied. "But I think you're right it seems much more specific in one direction now."

"OK," Will broke in, "Tomorrow we head in the direction of the gunshots we hear now,

Everyone agreed?"

"Yep" said Coop.

"Yep" answered Henry.

"Good, decision made! Whew, finally." Will declared. "Besides, I think there's something wrong with this stupid compass."

They could still hear the gunshots faintly and it seemed as if the gunshots were coming from one direction now. Listening to the gunshots that night was a haunting reminder of a world beyond their immediate reach; they clung to the hope that someone out there was getting closer to finding them.

Chapter Ten

WALK ABOUT AND GETTING OUT

As the first light of dawn appeared on the horizon, the boys found themselves caught between the fading darkness of the night and the uncertainty of a new and challenging day. The snow-covered landscape bore no traces of their journey, erasing the already faint footprints in the frozen ground. Even though it was taught when you were LOST to stay put and wait for a rescue group to find you and not get lost further, the boys did not want to stay and wait for that. They also were not sure of course, how long that could take and felt like they had no choice but to find their own way out. So, they decided they would be the heroes of their own story and choose their own destiny, they would make decisions as men and walk out in the direction of the gunshots heard all night. By morning, the boys felt confident about which direction to go. (Gunshots were less by early morning because only a few men kept shooting into the early morning and they held the same position as they were shooting so the direction was easier for the boys to pinpoint.)

Will, felt responsible that they were lost and unprepared and assessed the situation with a mix of determination and caution. He was the one that invited them to go with him, he should have been more prepared and attentive to details. The wolf encounter had added a layer of complexity to their predicament. As the new day unfolded, the trio, now facing more of the harshness wilderness, felt they faced a pivotal moment. The thought of becoming disoriented in the vast Alaskan wilderness had always been a lingering fear, and now it was a chilling reality. Would they still be lost for another night? The choices they made in the hours ahead would determine whether they emerged from this frozen expanse or became one with the untamed Alaskan landscape, possibly half-eaten or frozen.

"OK, we took a vote last night and we are all in favor of walking out and not waiting, right?" Will repeated.

"When lost, you are supposed to stay put, but I would rather try and get us out of here and not spend another night here with no water, food or warmer coat." Henry agreed.

"I agree too." said Cooper. He had rabbit blood all over his face and the other two didn't notice yesterday. And it was a bit humorous by morning like a movie scene.

Will felt a little more confident with Cooper's new look. He looked like a man that had been through hell and survived.

Will's clothes were shredded, and he had melted shoes. Henry had dirt on his face like he did it on purpose and none of them looked pretty, but they had each other. They were grateful they weren't alone.

Will checked the fire, "The wood is basically gone. That wolf made us use more wood than we would have needed." He remarked.

"I am gonna go look at the wolf tracks and see if we can figure out if there really was more than one wolf last night." Henry announced.

"Good idea," said Coop, "I'll come too."

"Don't walk through the tracks you guys, it will confuse you." Yelled Will after them.

"Ya, Ya, I know," answered Henry. "Maybe there were two, "said Henry, "the tracks going around the camp circle and back into the woods are confusing, but I am gonna say there were two of them."

"Gut Pile is gone!" yelled Will from a distance.

"Told ya!" responded Coop, "He found the gut pile and wanted more!"

Will caught up to them. "Pile is all but gone and he ate some fur, or something took some fur not sure, but it was all gone!"

Then Cooper spoke up, "I know I slowed you guys down yesterday and my cramps are only going to get worse, but if we do walk out of here just know that you will get a 110% out of me. I don't care what we do, I am sticking with the team and that is my only requirement – we stick together."

"OK, let's go! And we are going in the direction of the most gunshots last night not what the compass is showing." Will confirmed.

"Exactly," said Henry "and of course it's still cloudy, what dumb luck."

The trio made sure the backpack was with them, and guns were checked and loaded. As much good as they thought that would do, but that was all they had.

The trio clung to their rifles, it was their only defense against the known and unknown perils that lurked between them and safety. The wolf, though momentarily deterred, left an indelible mark on their minds. The idea of more than one wolf silently encircling them in the shadows fueled their anxiety as they headed out.

There was just enough light to be able to be sure there were no animals lurking nearby. However, all their eyes were circling and scanning nervously but none of them would talk about their fears aloud. The campfire lay smoldering as they hiked away from the camp, and it was a haunting reminder of the night's struggles and their world still beyond their reach.

The once familiar terrain now bore an unfamiliar edge. Each step became deliberate, and the crunching of snow beneath their feet felt like a reminder of their vulnerability.

Henry trying to lighten the mood spoke up, "Ya, know I hear they find people frozen to death in the woods and they have stripped all their clothes off."

"What? No way," Cooper shot back.

"Yea," Henry continued, "I guess hypothermia sets in and your body pulls in all of the blood from your extremities to keep your vital organs working and you start to feel such a heat surge that you strip all your clothes off, until you're naked. Can you believe that? You actually feel warm right before you die of hypothermia. I read it in more than one book."

"Ya, it's true, my dad has talked about that a few times." said Will "It's in a few different books and crazy true stories of the wilderness."

They each in turn started joking about what the kids at school would think when they heard that they found all three of them naked and huddled together. Cooper screamed, "Ewww, there is no amount of cold that would get me to do that."

"It didn't stop you last night," Henry chortled, and the other two shook their heads with laughter because it was funny, but it was tough keeping up their spirits and there wasn't a lot of energy for it. They were trying, Will thought, and he felt better about their chances. They didn't have to laugh at the jokes but if they were making them then they had a better chance.

But then again what would it matter? The boys had read a story about men who died in Alaska of hypothermia, it was a common tale. What could possibly be next to have to worry about, Will made a mental checklist of the challenges facing them: (1) a huge bear (2) a pack of wolves, (3) freezing to death, (4) dying from dehydration / exhaustion, (5) getting separated, which was the scariest one for Will, (6) frost bite setting in, especially on Henry and Will's tennis shoe covered feet, and (7) he couldn't remember seven. He thought he had counted seven. Oh yeah, a gun going off in a panic and shooting each other.

Cooper paused a second and took a deep breath. He was fighting back tears. They all were. They were scared to death, cold, hungry and exhausted. He righted himself by straightening his back, and then chortled, "I bet they find you two naked and cuddling together."

Henry and Will both genuinely laughed, but only for a second. It was a little too accurate right now to find them funny. Suddenly, Henry raised his gun and the other two jerked up their guns pointing in the same direction. A rabbit sprung across the thicket they were crossing.

"Geez Henry, don't do that," Will admonished him and released a lung full of air.

"Sorry guys, muscle memory, plus I'd be lying to you if I told you I didn't think that it was that stupid bear." Henry answered.

"Geez, you scared the Bageebaas out of me" Coop said, "and I don't have much Bageebaas left."

It was apparent that the brown bear was not their main problem, and they needed to start covering more distance or else face freezing to death. Will didn't know which would be worse, freezing to death or being eaten by a bear. He decided he didn't want to find out – he just wanted to be home out of the dark, out of the snow, and away from whatever beast lurked in the darkness.

He bit his lip, and he could taste blood now, but it was helping him fight off tears. A young boy that wants to be a man must learn tricks, so they don't cry in front of people, you can't have that.

He heard a kerplop and it snapped him out of thought. Will turned to see Henry jogging back to Cooper who had fallen over in the snow.

"Aaaaah, Cramp!" Cooper said through clenched teeth. Cooper rubbed his thigh furiously to relieve the cramping.

"Geez, I hate those." Will sympathetically replied. "I get those during football games and drop like a rock rubbing my calves out. Eat more snow, we don't have anything else. Have you been eating any snow?"

"He needs more than snow, Will." Henry whispered under his breath feeling overwhelmed.

A few minutes later they were walking again, and as they hiked up a large hill trying to push through with their guns, rabbits, heavy feet and heavy hearts it was a struggle and Cooper went down again. This time rolling and he dropped his gun and grasped his right thigh.

Will and Henry rushed to Cooper's side pushing his gun aside as they grabbed his right leg and started rubbing and stretching it out. It took several minutes and while he was stretched out Henry shoved snow at Cooper, he needed liquids and lots of them. The snow wasn't doing it and there was no going back.

Henry suddenly shouted, "I've got it. Why didn't I think of this before?"

"What Henry, out with it," Will said excitedly.

"Let's share carrying his gun," Henry said. That will relieve him of weight, and he should be able to move a little better with his hands free.

"That is your brilliant plan," Cooper said unimpressed. "Uh, no way, I am carrying my own gun."

Henry reexplained his reasoning, "We are in a bad spot, and we are going to have to do whatever we need to do to get out of here today. That includes sucking up our pride. That includes carrying each other or their stuff as far as we need too." Henry blurted out.

Will grabbed Cooper's gun and yelled, "I got it, let's go! Dark comes early and we need to make time."

They helped him to his feet. But he fell again before the top of the hill by slipping over a smaller dead fall. Will's heart froze when he saw him fall. Cooper jumped up as quickly as he could. "I'm fine, I got it. Don't worry."

Will was thinking they were losing it. Cooper was cramping up every quarter mile, and especially on the snow covered, slippery steep hills. Will couldn't blame him and had hidden his own minor cramps. He wondered if Henry was doing the same. They needed water in a bad way, they were constantly eating snow now, grabbing handfuls every few steps and they were getting worse not better. Then it hit him we need to find a lake. They hadn't seen one in miles, but they were everywhere out here, they just needed to find ONE.

Chapter Eleven

DINNER BELL OF BLOODY RABBITS

The challenging terrain—deadfall, tundra, and thick brush—were tripping them up, weariness and dehydration was setting in on all of them now. Cooper experienced cramping frequently, momentarily halting their progress. Henry questioned the wisdom of eating snow, wondering if it would make them colder. Dehydrated, hungry, thirsty, and fatigued, they grappled with the physical toll of their unplanned escapade.

Will adjusted the two guns numerous times in his hands trying to figure out how to keep his hands warm carrying cold metal guns.

"Give me a sec to adjust these guns." Will said and as he was looking down to adjust and pick up Cooper's 22, he noticed brown bear tracks again and saw more scat. The first thought that went through his head was to look around and be sure the bear wasn't nearby, but the next thought was, there was no way he wanted to spend another night in the woods.

When they left camp that morning Will wanted to leave the backpack of bloody rabbits. No one cared about the rabbits anymore, but they were all wondering if they may have to eat them another night. The thought was overwhelming. Will put the backpack on and tried not to think about whether any predator could smell the rabbits on him or would follow the boys because of the rabbits. He also thought he should be the one with the burden; besides he had the gun with the bear slug. A brown bear could smell them, he was sure of it. Was this bear following a blood trail, his last meal before hibernation? He knew the bears were supposed to be afraid of humans but that was not always the case and now Will probably smelled like those bloody rabbits. He had to hold on to the thought of the bear being normal and afraid of humans and he kept moving.

"Let's detour just a little maybe not panic like yesterday, I am getting too tired to panic and the tracks don't look fresh!" mumbled Henry.

"Good," responded Coop, "Detour sounds good, maybe there won't be as much deadfall to trip over."

Will announced "This backpack of bloody rabbits is making me nervous now that I know that wolf ate the gut pile and I am wearing them like a piece of bacon,"

As they were walking Will just kept thinking about bears and all the things he knew about them. He wished he could stop thinking about them, but the facts and memories just kept coming. Bears were most likely to be seen early morning and late evening. Bears live up to 30 years. He was taught that you don't leave food near your tent, put it 200 feet away minimum or hang it if you are hunting and came prepared.

Will started to recount a story to make noise again as they walked through the woods.

"Do you guys remember the Brown bear my grandpa shot in the driveway in his boxer shorts 2 years ago? The tagged bear?" Will questioned. "The story was in the Clarion paper."

"I do" answered Coop. "I was at your house later that day when the fish and game guy was there picking it up and he showed us the tag on his ear."

"Ya, do you remember him showing us how they looked up the number of the tag and

Could tell us he had been moved 3 times because he was a problem?"

"I forgot about that" responded Coop.

"Why was he at your house near the porch?" questioned Henry.

"He was looking for trash." Answered Will. "I watched that bear swing his head, snap his teeth and start huffing and woofing. It was freaky to watch.

I had never seen anything like it before. Then he jumped up and down on his front feet threatening us. His ears went back, and he started towards the porch where we were standing, and my grandpa shot him. He was still warm when the fish and game guy got there."

"It was awesome to see it up close like that." added Cooper.

"My dad is supposed to take me bear hunting next year." Henry said.

"I've had dreams about that bear." Said Will giving a little shake to throw off the thought.

"You guys know that a surveyor was killed right here last week." Said Cooper, "They think he took a bear by surprise."

"Do you think it's our bear? I mean the bear whose tracks we keep seeing?" replied Will.

"What was he surveying out here?" Will continued.

"Oil field stuff out here, I guess." Responded Cooper.

"I guess I heard about it." Henry said, "My dad was fixing his three-wheeler at his shop, I didn't pay that much attention to it at the time. Too tired and distracted by football practice to care."

"I did hear my mom ask my dad something about the location of that attack and questioning where we were going today. I didn't think much of that either." "WOW, I bet my mom is freaking out right now." Henry shook his head a bit feeling for his mom.

"My dad was talking to my grandpa about that at the homestead this week," added Cooper. "Fish and Game supposedly came and shot the bear responsible, or did they? How would we know?" They all went silent.

Then Will decided even with all the doubt pulling at them to give a pep talk. He snapped out of his thought about the bear and started in.

"Bloody rabbits or no bloody rabbits, how do you want to be remembered? Huh,

Cooper? Henry? How do you want to be remembered after this ordeal? Do you want everyone, friends, girlfriends, our families to see us as lost boys who needed rescuing?

How is that gonna feel? Or do you want them to remember you as men who took a wild adventure and scratched and clawed their way out of an Alaskan blizzard through brambles and the wild by themselves despite all the odds and the wild animals.

We have a chance to be heroes, our own heroes. So, what will it be? Do you want to be remembered as needy boys, or as brave and capable men who conquered the Alaska wilderness together? Besides, we may need these darn bloody rabbits one more time."

Will was trying to make himself feel better about carrying the rabbits.

"I can't stand the thought of being out here for another night." said Henry.

"I don't want to say I was lost and someone else had to help me because we are too stupid to figure out how to get out of here." Cooper chimed in. "There is no way I want to sit here and wait for the unknown."

"OK, me too." said Will, "Let's go." Will quickly adjusted the guns, and they all kept walking.

Chapter Twelve

A REBEL BUSH PILOT

John was a tough old timer and had been a bush pilot for 40 years. He was currently running through the snow, and he was rounding the final corner to the shop where his super cub airplane was parked for the winter. A phone call had just come through they were desperate for air support to rescue some local boys that had been out hunting and were lost. It was believed that the boys were not far from his hangar. Out near Swanson River Rd between Mosquito Lake and Finger Lake. John knew what that was like. He had been lost a few times as a young boy and knew the terror of it.

He grabbed the spare key hidden on the moose antlers outside the shop and let himself in. He pulled the fuel can over to the super cub and began filling it. All the way to the top – he would need as much as it was going to take if he was going to find those boys.

It was a two-seater, and there was no way to pick them up, especially in this weather. But he was good on the radio and trained in search and rescue protocol. He grabbed a survival pack from the back lockers and threw it in the back of the plane. They had informed him that the Civil Air patrol would not fly due to weather conditions. Well, he knew those boys were in a bad situation and he was going to do everything in his power to help them get out. He was also told they did not know the condition the boys were in after being out all night.

He was going to fly through this blizzard, he had done it before, he hoped to be able to fly low which was going to be risky. It didn't matter anyway, God had poked him, even seemed to be speaking to him, and he was called to it. He had never seen anything more clearly in his life and his whole body was smiling. Those boys were going to be alright, or he was going to die trying.

The physical toll on the boys was evident—torn gloves, blistered toes, dehydration, hunger, and melted shoes bore witness to their arduous journey. Yet, with the resilience of youth, they forged ahead, fueled by the hope that they would soon be reunited with their worried families and a meal. The pace was slower now. The boys were scanning the area for predators and going a bit slower to keep from cramping. Aware they were all struggling and getting very cold Will decided to throw the 22 down into the woods and just keep walking.

"I am chucking this gun you guys; we can come back for it" Will told the other two. One less thing to carry with cold hands and he could come back with his dad later and get it .... maybe. "You can have my

.22 Coop if we don't come back and get this." My grandpa has another one I can use."

"Fine." said Cooper making no objection. He would worry about it later.

Henry also made no objection. He agreed, "Good idea maybe the next time we come hunting over here we can find it." Henry thinking to himself that he didn't want to hunt rabbits for a long time after this expedition.

They had seen more rabbits, but no one wanted any more. Besides they were not going to spend another night out here or carry any more rabbits or leave a gut pile that a bear or wolf could use to follow them out.

Will was spent and he was falling behind as he stopped to take a leak. He called up to the other two, yelling, "just a second guys," as they rounded a small hill and disappeared. Those two were moving faster than he expected. They had decided to head toward the sounds of the gunfire but take the easier routes around the steep hills, because Cooper wasn't going to make it over any more deadfall.

Instantly, terror shot through Will, and he felt more alone than he ever had before. "Hey, wait up!" he yelled again, "hey wait up, guys!" A loud noise behind him spooked him and he turned pointing his gun, gulping in breaths and swinging the gun around.

Then the sound again, but this time he was listening. It wasn't a bear; it wasn't even a person – it was a plane. A distant rumbling in the sky brought the small plane and with it some hope. The aircraft circled overhead, the sight of it caused a rollercoaster of emotions. When it initially continued its path, disappointment set in, but then, miraculously, it returned for a second pass. Could it see them? He thought wildly.

"Hey, hey guys, wait up, look up!" he was screaming wildly.

"Hey, we need to wave it down," he yelled to everyone and no one. Then he sprinted off towards Cooper and Henry. They had picked up their pace and had obviously heard the plane. As a large lake appeared 100 yards in the distance before them without deadfall or a tricky climb in their way – a straight shot Will took off sprinting toward the boys and the lake. They had forgotten about a drink of water for a moment in time.

At this point, Henry was already running through the deep snow, high kneeing like a linebacker through a line of tires. Will was impressed and intensified his pace and copied the high knees. Henry reached the lake as the plane passed again a third time doing circles ever further away from the lake. Will was seconds behind him now and Henry got to the lake edge like he had been preparing for this moment all his life, removed his jacket in stride, his hat as well, and was waiving them around like a crazy fool. Screaming "Hey, here we are, over here, Hey, we're here!"

He might just wave that plane down, Will hoped.

Cooper and Will followed suit and started waving their ripped and destroyed coats over their heads, just like you see in the movies. It was surreal and time stood still.

The plane tipped its wings as if to say "hello" or "I see you." While completely exhausted they doubled their screaming and waiving. Sadly, and despairingly they watched the plane suddenly turn going south and disappear away from their sight again. The trio dropped, shoulders slouching, and Cooper let himself fall over flat in the snow in despair and exhausted.

"Nooooo," yelled Cooper.

"Where did he go?" Will asked noticeably confused and upset. He was too exhausted to cry.

Henry kicked at the snow, sending a puff of it up into the wind. "We are goners without that plane."

"They couldn't land anyway," Cooper broke in.

"Yea, but they could drop us a lighter," Henry said as if it was obvious. "A big red parachute with a blow torch on it and three Big Mac's with fries."

"Hey, he's coming back around," Will yelled. "Hey!" they all jumped and started swinging their jackets and hands again. The plane zoomed low tipped its wing and circled south once again.

"He saw us!" yelled Coop.

"Ya, what's he doing?" Henry questioned.

The boys, waving and jumping frantically, received the signal they desperately needed – go south. He was telling them to go south. Again, confusion but the signal seemed so exact. He kept circling and going south hoping they would catch on.

"Hey, I think he wants us to go that way" Will pointed south in the direction the plane went.

"What?" said Coop

"Ya, he keeps going that way and I think he's trying to tell us the path back." Will explained.

"Geez, can that be right?" Henry thought for a second, "Well, we weren't positive which way the gunshots came from last night anyway. Could we be going the wrong way again?"

"Let's go!" Will said and started moving that way. The other two followed.

Following the plane's directional cue, the boys ventured southward, praying that they correctly interpreted the message. Soon after, a rustling in the woods brought forth Cousin Zach who came barreling into sight with a glorious grin on his face, yelling, "Over here, over here!" The plane had brought the rescuers towards the lost boys and the lost boys towards the rescuers to meet in the middle!

Rifles were dropped and excited screams could be heard. Zach was just about knocked over by their greetings and hugs of delight.

"Oh, Glorious day!" yelled Henry.

"Yeeha!" screamed Cooper.

Zach emptied out his backpack and threw protein bars at the boys. Will had never tasted something so good. Next, Zach grabbed a small propane tank and lit it and let the boys warm their hands and feet. They were going to celebrate, and Zach informed them "We are only a mile from the road. You guys are almost out." They didn't care at that moment, they had Zach, they had food, they had heat, and even better they knew how to get out of here.

Zach pulled extra sets of gloves out of his bag for Will, as the other two didn't need them, and then he revealed three pairs of woolen socks. As he showed the boys, an Awwww like sound escaped each of their lips. "I have never seen someone so beautiful Zach," Cooper hugging him exclaimed! "I am so glad I don't have to spend another night out here."

Henry started howling like a coyote worshipping the moon as the reality set in, it was over the ordeal was over and they made it! All three of them made it!

"OOOOW, OOOOW!"

The setting was spectacular. Will smiled as he watched Henry celebrate and Cooper grabbing Cheez-its from Zach. His eyes started to well up with tears, and he didn't care, he wouldn't hide them. They had done it, and he deserved a nice relieving cry.

Moments later Patrick, and Bob, crashed through the trees to reunite with the lost trio too. The joy was indescribable and the relief on both sides immeasurable. When the boys learned later that the professional rescue crew got turned around and circled back to where they started, the boys felt less upset about their own misfortune. As Gatorade, snacks, a fire and dry socks brought relief the tale of their misadventure unfolded. The trio recounted details about the night of survival, the strange broken compass, the wolf sighting, the bear sign, and the challenging decision to abandon their gun and not sit still to be rescued but brave the wilderness together. They revealed more to the men about their brave souls then they realized.

After a bit refreshed and rejuvenated, the boys began the final leg of their adventure, flanked by Zach and their dads.

The boys soon appeared one by one out of the dense woods and trees and heavy brush. They were splattered in rabbit blood, soot-covered with shredded clothes, cut hands, melted shoes and gloves with the look of exhaustion on their faces, but radiated relief and joy. A welcoming committee consisted of paramedics, ambulances, horses, and a gathering of friends and family, all eager to witness the safe return of the intrepid trio. It was a beautiful sight to see. A happy ending. The cheers and applause of the onlookers greeted them. The trio had no idea what a big group had been waiting for them and what went on all night to secure a safe return for all of them. Their return marked the end of a harrowing journey and the beginning of a tale that would be retold for years to come.

***

This book is based on a true story. October 1997

Written by S. Kelly Reilly with input and comments from Todd Brigham, Brandon Huhndorf, Patrick Reilly, and Josh Reilly Esq. ©1998 the real boys of the Alaska Lost boys Adventure. Names were changed for the story.

Final note, the brave bush pilot that flew to their rescue during the blizzard and the next day is a real hero in this story though his part is small. He was called in by a friend of the family. Against the odds, fighting the weather and the FAA. Bill Michaels flew to the boys' rescue and did find them waiving their coats on that frozen Alaska lake flying in circles in the direction of Zach Reilly who did spend all night searching for the boys in a blizzard, who sprinted to their rescue on that cold lake embankment. Brandon did suffer from leg cramps and injuries. Todd suffered minor abrasions, and blistered toes from staying so close to the fire. Josh suffered an abrasion to his face, and abdomen, as well as frost bite on his right hand. In the exact spot the fingers on his glove were burned off. The large brown bear in that area where the boys were lost did kill a surveyor two weeks later in the location, they camped for the night the story of the surveyor was in the Peninsula Clarion newspaper. There also was a brown bear who was shot in Josh's grandfathers' yard, a tagged problem bear and picked up by Fish and Game. This article was a true story and featured in the Peninsula Clarion. The Peninsula Clarion on October 19, 1997, posted the article of the lost boys with a title of "Hunters found."

The bear's tracks seemed to follow them wherever they went those two harrowing days. Brandon, Josh, and Todd are still friends to this day and look back on this adventure with admiration for each other, and fond respect for the way that they each handled the situations as it got worse and worse. They rallied to each other's side. Kept going through the weather and obstacles both mental and physical.

In more jovial news, Todd really did drop his Charleston Chew and Josh did pick it up and eat it without telling him until after they were saved. Todd laughed once he heard what Josh had done. Josh felt bad, but not bad enough to say he would have done it any different.

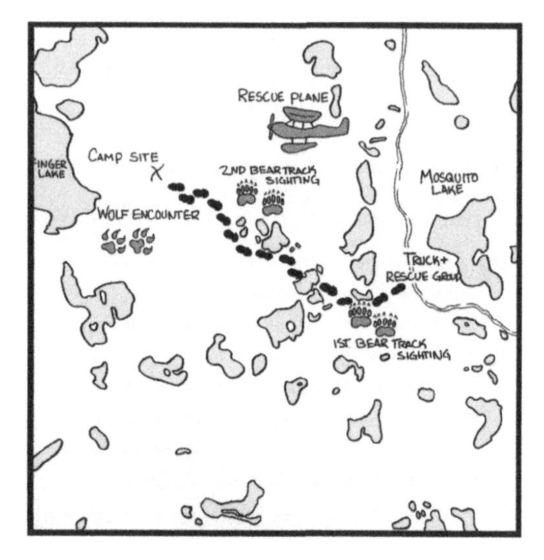

Chapter Thirteen

TEACHER BONUS SECTION FOR ALASKA LOST

BOYS ADVENTURE

What to expect from the Alaskan Wilderness

Types of Bears

To determine if a bear is a brown bear, a grizzly, or a black bear a few things will help you quickly. Remember, if you run a moose won't chase you far but a bear will!

Black Bears:

Black bears have straight backs compared to other types of bears. The ears are tall and more pointed than that of the brown bear. The claws are 1.5 inches long. Black bears are in most of the United States, Canada, and Mexico. Male black bears travel 300 square miles for their territory and females about 50 square miles. Black bears in general are intelligent and outnumber brown bears.

Black bear paws are smaller than grizzly claws in size, claws, and pads. Black bears climb trees, grasp branches, and dig for food with their smaller claws just as efficiently as brown bears. They are not as adapted for digging but climb trees and dig their dens all the same.

Brown Bears and Grizzly Bears:

Brown bears and grizzly bears are the same bear but have different diets. Grizzly bears are inland animals meaning they live in the interior parts of Alaska. Brown bears live close to the coast and eat fish. The fish are available from June to September in huge numbers. Both species eat a variety of grasses, roots, berries, and small animals likerabbits and squirrels.

Brown bears and grizzly bears have a large distinct shoulder hump. Their ears are round and short. They are typically brown but can range from cream to almostblack fur and still be a brown bear or grizzly. They can stand up to 8 feet tall. Their claws are 4 inches long and the face profile is more distinct than that of a black bear.

Long spread-out curved claws are used for many things including climbing trees and digging for food such as insects or squirrels. They also use them very efficientlyfor holding large salmon to eat or digging a winter den. Brown bears and grizzly bears have toes that provide traction and stability on snow, ice, and rocky surfaces.

Female brown bears/grizzlies give birth to 1-4 cubs and the cubs remain with their mothers for 2-3 years before going out on their own. A brown bear/grizzly is believed to have a better sense of smell than a dog, which is important to the story here.

Brown bears and grizzly bears face the threat of habitat loss due to human habitation.

Grizzly bears live in Montana, Wyoming, Idaho, Washington, Alaska, and Canada.

South of Canada, grizzlies are protected and are on the endangered species list.

Male grizzlies have 200-600 square mile territories, and the female range is 50-300 square miles.

Bears hibernate for 4-7 months starting in the fall depending on the weather, temperature, and food. They come out in April or May again depending on the weather. In warmer coastal places like Kenai, Alaska bear hibernation is very often only 4 months.

A bear den can be under roots or rocks, in a cave, or inside a log or tree. The dens are very small, so do not be deceived. If you run into what may appear to be a den leave it alone and get away, the bear may be back. However, they don't always use the same den winter after winter.

Polar Bears:

Polar bears live in the Arctic regions of Alaska, Russia, Greenland, Canada, and Norway. Polar bears are white, so they blend in with their environment. Polar bears have 2 layers of fur to stay warm and these bears have webbed front paws for swimming. They build their dens in snow and ice. They have longer necks than brown bears and grizzly bears. A polar bear's vision is similar to ours, but they can find the breathing hole of a seal by its scent. As you may have guessed, their hearing is better than a human. Polar bears can live around 30 years.

Also, in case you were wondering, polar bears and penguins do not live in the same areas.

Wolves

Wolves are seen as a spirit of the wild and wilderness. A Kenai wolf is called a gray wolf or timber wolf.

Wolves' habitats include forests, tundra, and mountains. They have thick fur and range from gray to black with variations of that depending on where they live. Wolves communicate through howling, barking, and growling. Wolves are carnivorous and eat meat. Their diet in Alaska includes moose, caribou, Dall sheep, muskoxen, and small mammals like rabbits, mice, voles, and squirrels.

A pack is a family group with a dominant breeding pair and their offspring. There can be a few members of a pack or over a dozen. There are usually 4-6 pups in a litter and they are born in dens in the spring. Both parents and the pack help raise and care for the pups. Lots of pack members participate in raising the pups. Parents, grandparents, teachers, and many other wolf adults help, much like human children.

Wolves are a huge part of maintaining balance in an ecosystem. They control populations of herbivores and help prevent overgrazing of vegetation.

If approached by a wolf, DO NOT RUN, use eye contact, and act aggressively. Retreat slowly, stand your ground, and fight with sticks, rocks, or bear spray. Climb a tree! Wolves can't climb but bears can.

Rabies is also a concern. Wolves usually avoid humans unless you are near their kill.

Wolves can go for days without food and will prey on other wolves. They can also die of malnutrition, disease, hunting, and trapping.

A coyote is smaller and has a skinny nose and tall pointed ears. They are usually much thinner in their body than the wolf. The coyote has smaller paw prints and a bushier tail.

The wolf's tail is shorter and much thicker than a coyote's. Both compete for the same prey.

Moose

Moose can weigh between 800-1600 lbs. Their calves are normally born during the first part of May in Alaska. They also have antlers, not horns. Antlers regrow every summer and the males fight in the fall during mating season and then the antlers fall off. Their life span can be up to 16 years. They live in Alaska, North America, Europe and Russia.

Rabbits and Snowshoe hares

Rabbits in Alaska are called... you guessed it "Snowshoe hares." They are called jackrabbits in the summer. The Alaska Snowshoe can weigh more than a regular rabbit. They weigh up to 12 pounds while regular hares are closer to 4 pounds. Regular rabbits or cottontail rabbits live in Southeast Alaska, the environment is better for them. They are smaller, skinnier, they have shorter legs, and their babies are born hairless and blind. The Snowshoe hares or Jackrabbits are larger, have larger ears, they are faster and live above ground in nests they do not burrow. They weigh up to 12 lbs. as compared to a 4lb. Rabbit. Snowshoe hares have babies born with their eyes open and hair on them at birth.

The Tundra

The Alaska tundra is mostly gently rolling hills, with low vegetation such as mosses, lichens, grasses, and small shrubs. The ground is often covered with a layer of permafrost, which is permanently frozen soil, making it difficult for plants to establish deep root systems. Trees can't dig deep roots in part of Alaska so high winds can knock over a tree creating the "rootball shelter" in the story. The boys were lost in the fall. As the story unfolds, and you see that lack of preparation greatly affected them.

Fall in the tundra can be unpredictable, with rapidly changing weather conditions. Temperatures can fluctuate widely, ranging from below-freezing to above-freezing during the day. Cold winds and occasional snowfall are common, adding to the challenges of traversing the land.

The tundra is dotted with wetlands, ponds, and bogs, which make walking difficult and treacherous. These saturated areas are often covered with mosses and sedges and may be concealed by a thin layer of vegetation, making it easy to accidentally step into them. It is full of low wet spots and very uneven ground for walking.

When walking through the tundra in the fall, it is essential to be prepared for changing weather conditions and challenging terrain. Wear layers of clothing to stay warm and dry, sturdy footwear with good traction to navigate uneven ground, and carry essential supplies such as food, water, a map, and a compass or GPS device. Additionally, let someone know your plans and the time you expect to return in case of emergencies. But beware cell phones may not work in many areas you may want to explore.

Permafrost

Permafrost is permanently frozen ground even in the summer of Alaska. Trees and bushes cannot establish deep root systems.

The tundra undergoes a dramatic transformation in the fall as temperatures drop and daylight hours decrease. The vibrant colors of summer foliage give way to a gold and brown and russet palette as plants prepare for winter dormancy. Some species of plants may begin to senesce and wither, while others display vibrant autumn colors before shedding their leaves. Permafrost underlies much of the tundra landscape. It creates a solid, uneven surface that can be challenging to navigate, especially when the tundra becomes even more frozen and rigid, making it harder to walk on.

Animals that live in Alaska on the tundra and in the woods are caribou, musk ox, great horned owls, bald eagles, hawks, beavers, river and sea otters, porcupines, muskrats, squirrels, voles, mice, shrews, coyotes, wolves, bears, moose and weasels.

Other Dangers

Hypothermia is the state in which the body temperature goes dangerously low. The dangerous temperature for a body starts at 95 degrees. We are normally 98.7 so it doesn't sound like that much, but it is. Hypothermia can be mild or severe.

One of the symptoms of this is you cannot get warm easily and it can take a long time to recover your body heat. Another symptom is you begin to shiver. Another symptom is shallow breathing, and you can start getting confused. The boys in the story were taught about hypothermia and its last symptom: your body will release a massive heat surge to warm you, but it is so great and in the confused state people take their clothes off and they are often found naked and frozen. It can take a long time to get hypothermia depending on where you are, and who you are, young or old. Very cold-water temperatures can throw you into hypothermia almost immediately. Being educated about this can help you or someone you know, recognize it, and take the right action to get the person warm and know when to get help.

Chapter Fourteen

DISCUSSION for the Alaska Lost Boys Book

The book is based on the true story of three boys who learned about their environment, the animals living there, and ways to survive. Because many of us live away from the wild, this knowledge is almost lost. Children should be taught how to build a survival fire and forage for food in the area where they live and recreate. They should also learn about weather conditions and local wildlife in their area. This is a short quiz on the survival skills the boys were taught, apart from how to build the fire.

A project for young people and an exciting one for them is to learn about things that are edible in the different seasons in your climate and environment. Building a fire for survival and warmth is also very worthy. Understanding how animals live and eat and hunt where you live can be extremely interesting and teaches children the importance of the balance of nature. When you learn about your environment and become even slightly educated about these things fear is reduced. Even a minimal education of basic knowledge surrounding animals and survival should be a class in school. How many of us can even name the trees in our neighborhood?

Dandelions and Chamomile weeds, as we call them, are completely edible and easily recognizable! We must learn some of this to protect these habitats for the animals who live among us.

You probably already know many things that you don't realize you know about the place you live. Such as which animals live near you, and which animals are dangerous or friendly?

Which animals living near you are nocturnal?

Do you live in a desert or the mountains or a city?

Do you know what trees and bushes and flowers are in your state or city?

Do you know which ones could be edible?

Do you know the directions of North, South, East, or West standing in your yard?

What would you take with you if you hiked even for a few hours?

If you saw an animal that you are afraid of, what is the best way to handle a possible encounter?

Would you know what animals may be in the area you are hiking in?

Would you recognize tracks of animals in your area?

After reading the story what would you do different if you were lost?

What clothing in your area would you put on if you maybe had to spend a night lost?

Would you stick together as a team?

Would you check your compass before leaving?

Would you learn about shelter building in your area using what was available for where you would be hiking?

Would you bother with carrying extra socks or gloves or bandaids?

Would you drink from a lake or creek you were unsure about?

Do you know how to build a campfire?

If your cell phone did not have service in the area what else would you do?

Would carrying a whistle be helpful for you?

Would you stay put once you realized you were lost? Or would it depend on other circumstances what you would choose to do?

Chapter Fifteen

QUIZ

1 .What are some differences between a black bear and a brown bear?

A. A shoulder hump

B. Longer claws

C. Ear shape and length

D. Hibernation den

E. Food eaten

F. All of the above

2. How much does a brown bear weigh?

A. Up to 300 lbs

B. Up to 1200 lbs.

C. Up to 600 lbs.

3. How long does a bear hibernate in Alaska?

A. 1-2 months

B. 3 months

C. 4-7 months

4. What do brown bears eat in Alaska?

A. Berries

B. Fish

C. Honey

D. All of the above

5. Are brown bears and grizzly bears the same kind of bear?

A. Yes, except for their diet and where they live

B. No, they are different kinds of bears

6. Do wolves hunt solo or in a pack?

A. No, they hunt in packs

B. Yes, they hunt alone

7. Are coyotes and wolves the same thing?

A. No, coyotes are much smaller and skinnier

B. Yes, they are the same

8. Do rabbits live in Alaska?

A. Yes, but only in Southeast Alaska

B. No, only large Snowshoe hares

9. Do Snowshoe hares live in Alaska?

A. Yes and are Jackrabbits in the summer.

B. No, only rabbits.

10. Can you always depend on a cell phone if your lost?

A. No cell service may not be available

B. Yes, if it is charged.

11. What material do you need to start a survival fire?

A. tinder, kindling and firewood

B. kindling and firewood

C. tinder, kindling, firewood and matches

D. All of the above

12. What lights easier when starting a fire for survival?

A. tinder

B. kindling

C. firewood

13. What season do bears hibernate in Alaska?

A. Summer

B. Fall

C. Winter

D. Spring

14. If you run into a brown bear in Alaska, what should you NOT do?

A. Run

B. Play dead

C. Climb a tree

15. Which has the best nose for smell?

A. A bear

B. A dog

16. What can keep you safe from predators?

A. A backpack

B. A compass

C. A big fire

17. What is scat?

A. Scat is a bush in Alaska

B. Scat is an animal in Alaska

C. Scat is an animal's poop

18. Are snakes in Alaska?

A. No

B. Yes

19. When you're lost, what do you do so you are more easily found?

A. Stay put once you realize you are lost

B. Don't panic

C. Signal for help if possible

D. Make a fire

E. All of the above

20. Which bear has white fur?

A. Black bear

B. Grizzly bear

D. Brown bear

E. Polar bear

21. Which bear lives in the woods of Alaska?

A. Black bear

B. Brown bear

C. Grizzly bear

D. Polar bear

E. A, B and C

22. Which characteristic separates out the Snowshoe from the rabbit?

A. Ears, size, legs, region

B. Color of fur

C. Lives in a nest or a burrow

D. All of the above

23. What are some of the things wolves eat?

A. Berries

B. Caribou and Rodents

C. Honey

D. A and C

24. What things should you take on a hike even if it's short?

A. Pocket knife

B. Compass

C. Whistle

D. Lighter for a fire starter

E. Water or cup for drinking water

F. All of the above

25. The Beaver Fever virus includes what symptoms?

A. Fever

B. Diarrhea

C. Rash

D. Nausea

E. A, B, and D

26. What are some reasons to know the tracks of animals who live in your area?

A. To know if there is a dangerous animal near you by knowing his tracks

B. To find and play with the animal

C. To be able to be aware of your surroundings for safety

D. To know for fun that animals are near

E. A, C and D

27. When can you get hypothermia?

A. When you have the flu

B. In the heat

C. When you get too cold

D. After eating bad berries

28. What are some symptoms of hypothermia?

A. Fever

B. Cold and wet

C. Can't get warm

D. Shivering

E. B, C, and D

29. What is Tundra?

A. A city in Alaska

B. An animal in Alaska

C. A type of terrain in Alaska

30. What is a deadfall in Alaska?

A. A city in Alaska

B. A plant in Alaska

C. A dead tree fallen over

D. An Alaskan winter

About the author

Kelly was raised in Colorado and moved to Alaska with her husband, Patrick at age 19. They built a log cabin in the backwoods of Nikiski, Alaska and raised 4 kids. For a few years there was no plumbing, electricity or real windows. After some time Patrick became a contractor. He loved Alaska hunting and fishing, trapping, boat building and everything about it. Kelly became a photographer in Kenai Alaska and has always wanted to write children's books. This story is based on a true story about one of Kelly's boys and two close friends who became lost in the woods while rabbit hunting in a blizzard in Alaska. She has other children's books also.

Made in the USA
Las Vegas, NV
16 December 2024